Enduring Act

By H. D'Agostino

H. D'Agostino
Enduring Act
H. D'Agostino

Cover Design by Pink Ink Designs
Editing by Kellie Montgomery

Table of Contents

Chapter 1

Brooke

I struggled to open my eyes. I could hear beeping, but it was muffled. It's almost as if I had cotton in my ears. I don't know how long I've been here, days, weeks? Nothing makes sense. Where's my house, and Ava? Why is Blake a doctor and how did I get back here? Did Warren bring me back?

The room appeared blurry when I blinked against the muted light. My head was throbbing, but when I lifted my arm to touch the bandage, I was restricted. There are so many wires and tubes coming out of me, I can hardly move. I rolled my head slowly to the side. I'm alone. He left, but when? I needed to get out of here. Just as I struggled to sit up, I felt her. The baby's kicking me, hard. "It's ok. Mommy's going to keep you safe," I whispered as I caressed my swollen belly. How did she survive this? Why did he let her? My head continues to pulse as I close my eyes and fall back into the darkness.

ooooooooo

I don't know how long it's been, but when I open my eyes it's easier to see. Daylight streams through the window, and the city seems alive. I glanced to the right; the chair in the corner is still empty. I glanced to the left; there's a vase of flowers sitting on the small table. I don't remember anyone bringing me flowers. They're yellow. Warren used to use yellow flowers for his fake apologies. It makes my stomach roll to think about it.

Just as I'm attempting to call the nurse, there's a knock on my door. It slowly opens, and the nurse from the other day steps in. At least I think it was another day.

"Good morning, Brooke." She smiled as she came over to the machines. She pressed a few buttons before smiling at me again. "How are you feeling today?"

"Confused." I was honest.

"About what?" She clasped her hands in front of her.

"How did I get here?" I figured that was the easiest question to start with.

"Your husband brought you in. You fell down the stairs at home. He's been very worried. Hasn't left your side until last night." She straightened the sheets on the bed and fluffed my pillow.

"Where's Ava?" I grimaced as I shifted in the bed. It didn't make sense. Ava was five. She should be here.

"Whose Ava?" The nurse checked my chart.

"My daughter." I swallowed.

"I wasn't aware that you had any other children. Mr. Ellis said this was your first." She pointed to my stomach. I was still confused by how I got pregnant again. I haven't been with anyone.

"How long have I been here?"

"A little over two weeks." She put the chart back. "Are you ok?"

"No," I whispered. "I'm not ok. I'm not ok at all." I started to panic and the beeping on the machine sped up.

"You need to calm down, Mrs. Ellis. This isn't good for your head injury or the baby." She moved closer. "Do you want me to call your husband? Will that help you relax?"

"No." I attempted to shake my head, but the pain was too much and I started to get sick to my stomach. "Please don't," I begged.

"Are you in some kinda trouble?" The nurse leaned closer.

"He did this. He did this to me. He tried to kill me." I choked the words out as my head pulsed and my eyes closed in pain.

"You need rest, Mrs. Ellis. Let me give you something to help with that. My name's Donna. You push this button and call me if you need anything else." She squeezed a syringe of clear liquid into the IV and the blackness came back, swallowing me whole.

oooooooo

'I don't understand what's going on.' That thought has been on the edge of my mind since I first heard Warren's voice in the darkness. Have I really been here two weeks? When I woke up once again, the room was empty. The yellow flowers still sat on the table in the corner. Just seeing them there made me want to throw them across the room. I knew they were from him. He did this, and he wanted me to know it. The flowers were a way to make me remember that he was in charge. He wasn't physically here, but he was still in charge.

"Mrs. Ellis." Dr. Douglas slowly appeared from behind my door. "Good afternoon."

"Hi." I smiled weakly. My head still hurt, but some of the tubes had been removed so I could move a little better.

"How are you feeling today?" He slid the chair from the corner closer as he sat down.

"Ok, I guess." I sighed. I don't really know what he was expecting me to say.

"Nurse Donna said something about you being in trouble." His face turned serious. "Do you need help? If you need help, you can tell me."

I glanced at the yellow flowers in the corner of the room, mocking me. "I'm fine. It must have been the meds."

"Are you sure? She said you seemed really upset." He patted my arm.

"I'm sure." I pulled away. I knew if Warren happened to come in, he'd accuse me of cheating. I'd been there too many times before. Innocent friendships had cost me broken bones, cuts, and more insults than I care to remember.

"Well, you should be out of here in a few days. I'm sending your OB down to do your monthly exam this afternoon." He stood and placed my chart back in its holder.

"Thanks." I shifted, and it hurt. He must have seen me grimace because he stepped closer.

"Do you need something for the pain? Broken ribs can take a while to heal."

"I'm fine." I groaned. I'd been down this road before. "Thank you, Doctor."

"Call me Blake." He waved as he left.

Broken ribs? A brain injury? What else was I dealing with, and why couldn't I remember how this happened?

oooooooo

I managed to stay awake for most of the afternoon. It felt like an accomplishment since I'd been sleeping so much lately. When Dr. McGee came walking in, it was the first time

I felt like I wasn't going crazy. She'd been my doctor for years, and I remember her telling me I was pregnant.

"Hi, Brooke. It's good to see you awake." She closed the door as she stepped closer to the bed.

"Hi." I smiled back. "I'm so happy to see you." I reached for her hand. "I think I'm going crazy," I whispered. "Where's Ava?"

"Ava?" Dr. McGee's brow furrowed as she stared at me. "Who's Ava?"

"My daughter. She's five. You told me I was going to have her six years ago. Where is she?"

"Brooke," Dr. McGee lowered her voice, "this is the first baby that I've helped you with." She placed her hand on my swollen belly. "Are you ok? Did Warren do this?"

"Do what?" I started to panic. It was happening again.

"The last time I saw you, you told me he was hurting you. I gave you the name of a shelter you could go to. I was trying to help you. Did you try to leave?" She held my hand with genuine concern, but all I felt was anger. Was everyone here trying to make me believe that I was crazy?

"I did leave. Five years ago. I left. I went on the run. I had the baby. I was happy. Finally getting my life back, and he showed up." The words were flying out of my mouth so fast that I wasn't sure even I believed them anymore.

"I saw you six months ago, Brooke. That's when we discovered this little one was coming. You were here six months ago." She rubbed my arm, but I pulled away.

"No, I wasn't. I was on the other side of the country. He showed up and hurt me. He brought me back. Why doesn't anyone believe this?" The beeping on the machines began to speed up.

"You need to calm down. This isn't good for the baby," Dr. McGee soothed.

"I can't calm down. Nobody believes me." I began gasping for air. The room seemed to shrink, and as my eyes scanned the area, he showed up.

"Everything ok?" Warren stepped into the room, crossing his arms over his chest.

"Fine." I kept my answer short. I didn't need to give him any ammunition for convincing the doctors to lock me in the looney bin.

"I just need to measure her stomach, then I'll be all finished." Dr. McGee smiled, but I could tell she was trying to hide my outburst. She removed a soft tape measure from her lab coat pocket, and stretched it across my stomach. "Everything looks great. I'll be back by to check on you before you're discharged but I expect to see you in my office next month."

"I'll make sure she gets there." Warren smiled but I could tell it was forced. I watched Dr. McGee leave, and Warren take over the chair she was sitting in. He didn't say anything at first, just scooted impossibly close. "I see what you're doing," he whispered in my ear. "You're hoping one of them will save you. I don't know how many times I have to show you that I'm in charge," he growled. "This thing lived because I let it." He placed his hand on my stomach, causing me to flinch. "Whether it does next time depends on you." He leaned back and crossed his arms. "Like the flowers?" He lifted his chin and smiled. To anyone walking by, he would appear to be the loving husband. He played the role well, but I knew better. Warren was the nightmare that I couldn't seem to escape from no matter how hard I tried. I thought I'd put all of this behind me, but now I'm beginning to wonder if any of it was real.

Chapter 2

Brooke

The next five days went faster than I would have liked. Dr. Douglas was satisfied with my progress, so I was given the ok to leave. Fear gripped me when Warren was handed my discharge papers.

He'd shown up that morning, playing the role of loving husband. He'd pretty much demanded that I be released. Since my care was manageable, the doctors ok'd it. A nurse wheeled me down to the drop-off door where Warren was waiting with his car.

He smiled as he opened the door and I slowly lowered myself inside. After buckling up, he jogged around to his door and climbed in. I waved to the orderly as he rolled the wheelchair away, and swallowed the lump in my throat as the hospital disappeared in the distance. This was it. I was on my own again. My days would be determined by Warren's moods. My life would be propelled by fear.

We didn't speak the entire drive home. I was afraid of the response I'd get, and didn't want to upset him. I was still recovering, and couldn't really defend myself. As we pulled into the driveway, I saw a bag on the porch by the door. "Damn neighbors need to butt out," Warren grumbled as he climbed out of the car and slammed the door. I sat there hoping that he'd come around and help me, but he continued to walk toward the door. "You coming?" He threw his arms in the air as he looked at me from the steps.

Guess this was it. We weren't somewhere where he needed to put on a show, so I was back to doing it all for myself. I slowly pushed the door open. My side ached where my cracked ribs were. I swung my legs out, and used the seat to push myself to a standing position. I shuffled along until I reached the steps. Using the handrail, I climbed the steps achingly slow. "What's that?" I motioned to the bag that was sitting by the door.

Warren rolled his eyes. "The neighbors have been dropping off food for you. I guess they think you can't cook now."

"That was nice," I whispered.

"It's nosy," he grumbled as he lifted the bag and carried it inside. "There's all kinds of crap that they've brought over the last few days. Guess you're off the hook for a little while. Good for you, I guess." He shook his head as he unlocked the door, and went inside.

I stood there on the porch just letting the words sink in. Good for me? Did he really expect me to go on like nothing happened? I've been hospitalized for almost three weeks. Did that mean nothing? How could I have ever loved this man?

I sighed as I came inside the living room. There were newspapers scattered on the floor. A lamp was knocked over, and a hole in the wall next to the kitchen door glared back at me. "I got work to do." Warren waved his arm in the air as he stormed off toward his office. "Clean some of this mess up."

I blinked as I looked around in disbelief. It was a disaster zone everywhere I could see. I wandered toward the stairs only to see more destruction. A few books lay cluttered on the landing, another hole in the sheetrock, a spindle was missing on the railing, and a small puddle of dried blood was on the carpet at the base of the stairs. It looked like a crime scene, and for anyone who didn't live here it would be shocking. The sad thing was, this wasn't anything abnormal for me.

I knew that Warren had left this mess as a reminder. He wanted me to know that what happened was my fault, and he was in charge. I carefully climbed the stairs, placed my things in our room, and then went to the bathroom to grab cleaning supplies. Any other person would have laid down to rest, but I wasn't afforded that luxury. If I didn't do as I was told, he'd do it again. I wasn't sure how many more times I'd survive this, and based on what he said in the hospital… he'd make sure our daughter didn't.

ooooooo

It took me most of the afternoon to clean the living room and stairs up. I was constantly taking breaks to catch my breath. Too much exertion made me light headed, and my ribs ached every time I bent over. I couldn't repair the hole in the wall or the broken spindle, so those were left for Warren.

When I finally finished, I crept up the stairs to put away the cleaning supplies. Moments after I put the bucket in the bathroom, I heard the office door creak open. I sighed as I waited for what I knew was coming. I shuffled into the bedroom, and sat on the edge of the bed. I was exhausted, and just wanted to rest.

"Brooke!" Warren's voice echoed through the house. "I'm hungry. Come heat up something for dinner." I knew that if I didn't follow his commands, he'd be up here dragging me downstairs. The good news was I didn't have to actually cook anything. The neighbors had been a blessing in that aspect.

"Just a moment," I called out as loud as I could. It hurt to move. It hurt to yell. My head throbbed in protest as I stood and made my way to the stairs. I stood there at the top, just staring at them. I willed myself to remember what happened, but it was no use. No amount of pressure was going to help. Dr. Douglas had said that I might never get my memory back. In some ways, I hope he was right. I have enough nightmares from Warren to last me a lifetime. I don't need more.

When I reached the kitchen, Warren was sitting at the breakfast nook with his arms folded on the table. "Bout time," he grumbled as I opened the refrigerator. There had to be at least ten containers stacked on the shelves. "What would you like?" I turned to face him, and waited for an answer.

"Whatever is the quickest. I'm starving." He rolled his eyes. The urge to slap him was never more powerful, but I knew I couldn't. He acted like he was incapable of doing anything for himself. I can't believe that I've let him do this for years. There are parts of me that want away from this so bad, but there are other parts, the ones that keep me here, that are scared to leave. I've had Warren tell me what to do for so long, that I'm not sure I could function on my own.

"How about chicken?" I held up a container. "There are potatoes and broccoli in here too. That all goes together." I tried to smile even though I was measuring every word that left my lips. One wrong one, and I'd end up on the floor, cleaning this food up.

"Fine," he growled.

I carefully pulled down two plates, dished the food out, and placed one in the microwave. After setting the timer, I placed the containers back in the fridge. When the microwave beeped, I tested the food before carrying it over to Warren. After placing it in front of him, I heated up my own plate. "How's that?" I waited with bated breath for him to scream at me about something.

"Good. Glad to see that bump on the head didn't cause you to forget your place." He lifted his chin as he chuckled to himself. A small part of me broke that night. I'd always hoped that somewhere inside of him would be a decent man. I thought that if he hurt me bad enough, he might see the error of his ways, but this just proved that he didn't. He didn't care if he hurt me. Hell, I don't think he cared if he killed me.

We sat at the table in silence that night, quietly eating our dinner. When we finished, Warren stood and walked away, leaving the mess for me. I painstakingly cleaned the dishes, wiped down the counters, and then hobbled over to where we kept the medicine. After taking the pain pills I'd been sent home with today, I made my way to the bedroom.

When I reached our door, the lights were off. Warren was already asleep on his side of the bed. I fumbled through the dark, knowing that if I turned on the lights, I'd have hell to pay. When I caught my toe on the bed, I mashed my lips together to keep from crying out in pain. Night time preparations took twice as long as they should have, but when my body hit the soft mattress, I almost sighed. Being back home was hard, but at least I could sleep in my own bed. If I am being honest though, I don't know how much longer I can do this.

The idea of leaving has been growing stronger ever since Dr. McGee mentioned it. I need to leave again, only I need to find someone who remembers where I went. I can't have him finding me again, and I can't remember how I got there.

Chapter 3

Brooke

It's been a month since I came home. Not much has changed, but Warren hasn't physically hurt me. Ever since I came home, he's kept me on my toes though. I think he's playing some kind of psychological game now. I spend most of my days watching for him. He leaves in the morning, and I relax. Normally he comes home around six in the evening. I don't even need to look at the clock anymore. My body has trained itself to be on high alert. Right around five thirty, I can feel all the muscles tightening. Sometimes I even feel sick.

I'm supposed to see Dr. McGee this afternoon for my seven-month checkup. After today, I'll start going twice a month. I'm both excited and scared to have this baby. I'm worried what Warren might do once the baby's here, but I'm dying to meet her. Every time I feel her kick, I think about Ava. I wonder what Warren did to her; if she's ok or remembers me? No one seems to have an answer for me, but I know she was real. She had to be real.

Warren told me he was too busy to take me to the doctor today, so I had to get a cab. It was a short ride, and beautiful outside. Fall was in the air, and the crisp leaves crunched under my feet as I walked. The streets were lined with golds, oranges, and reds, and the sky was a bright blue. I felt like I was in the middle of a storybook as the breeze blew against my face.

oooooooooo

When I reached Dr. McGee's building, I paused. She said this was the first pregnancy she's helped me with, but I remembered coming here with Ava. Everything was the same. The building looked the same, even the flowers out front were the same. I rubbed my eyes as I tried to remember anything that would make me feel like I wasn't going crazy, but the harder I tried, the worse I felt.

The elevator ride was slow and when the doors dinged open, I was met with the familiar smell of the office. I signed in, and took a seat. The TV in the corner was turned down low but I could still hear the weather report predicting an early frost. I wasn't sitting long, before I was ushered back to a room. The nurse jotted a few things in my file before leaving me there on the paper covered table.

My eyes scanned the room, looking for clues to point out to Dr. McGee. She had to remember the last time. I only saw her a few times, but she was so persistent about me leaving. She had to remember. The harder I looked, the more my head throbbed, warning me to stop.

"Brooke." Dr. McGee smiled as she entered the room. "How are you today?"

"Ok, I guess." I shrugged. I honestly didn't know how I felt. My head still hurt on a regular basis, my ribs did too if I bumped them just right. No one believed me when I talked to them about leaving. "Confused, mainly."

"Confused how?" Dr. McGee sat down and patted my knee.

"You're going to think I'm crazy." I sighed as I glanced out the window at the sun. It was the one constant that I could rely on. It came up, and went down… never changing.

"You suffered a terrible head injury. Memory loss and confusion are normal," she soothed.

"This isn't memory loss," I growled. "I was here. Six years ago. I was here. I had a baby." My heart began to race as I balled my hands into fists.

"Brooke." Dr. McGee stood and stepped between me and my sight line.

"No!" I slammed my fists on the exam table. "I know I sound crazy, but I'm not. You helped me." Tears of frustration welled in my eyes as a vision of Ava's face floated through my mind. "He had to have taken her." I sighed.

"Who? Warren?" Dr. McGee's brow crinkled.

"Who else?" I closed my eyes and shook my head.

"Has he hurt you again?" The urgency in her voice startled me.

"You mean like hit me? No." I began to pick at my nails.

"I can help you, Brooke. I can help you leave. There are places for women like you. I have friends who work at these places. They'll keep you and the baby safe." She fumbled through the pocket of her lab coat until she produced a small white card. "Here." She handed it to me. "There's a number on the back. If you want to leave, call that number. We'll help you."

It was as if a movie was playing out in front of me. I've had this conversation before. It was almost exactly the same. "Don't you remember this?" I took the card. "You did this the last time I was here."

"I've helped several women over my time working here, Brooke. Sadly, you aren't the first." She frowned. "Let's get you measured, and we'll set up your next appointment."

"Fine," I mumbled. I was done trying to convince her of anything. It wasn't working, and I was wasting my breath.

ooooooooo

After leaving the office, I took a short walk to the coffee shop down the block. I ordered a tea, and sat by the window, people watching. The afternoon was slowly turning to evening, and a chill was beginning to form in the air. I should have gone straight home, but I didn't. I sat there just thinking. Thinking about my life, how things could be different, how things should be different, what it might be like if I was with someone other than Warren. I let my mind wander as I sipped my tea. I started daydreaming about Officer Blake and Ava. I thought about the house he fixed up for me and the treehouse he built for Ava. I thought about our time living at the beach and on the farm. All the sacrifices I made over the years, and the friends who knew nothing about me. Where were they all, and was it even real?

By the time I finished my tea, the sun was setting. I pulled my coat tighter around me as I walked along the sidewalk. I hailed a cab, and made the short ride home. When I climbed out of the cab, I noticed there were no lights on. Warren's car was in the drive, but it looked like no one was home. I assumed he was working in his office. I slowly climbed the front steps, fumbled in the dim lighting to get the door open, and then shuffled inside. I set my purse and coat on the edge of the couch, and flicked a light on.

"Where have you been?" his voice growled as he stepped around the corner.

I jumped as my hands flew to my chest. "You startled me."

"Where have you been?" He stepped closer, causing me to sidestep him.

"I had an appointment, remember?" I caressed my belly.

"Right, for that thing." He curled his lip in disgust.

"This thing is your daughter." Tears welled in my eyes as my voice shook. How could he be like this about his own child?

"I've been sitting here for an hour. It is way past dinner time. Your appointment was hours ago." His voice grew louder with each statement. "So, I'm going to ask you again… where have you been?" By this point he'd moved in front of me. I had my back against the closed door, and he was leaning inches from my face. I could smell the whisky on his breath, and it made me feel sick.

"I stopped for tea," I whimpered. I knew I just needed to be honest. He'd still be mad, but lying made it worse.

"Tea?! You were drinking fucking tea while I'm sitting here waiting on you?!" he bellowed.

"I'm sorry." I sobbed. "I'll fix something right now." I started to step around him but he grabbed my upper arm.

"You don't ever make me wait," he growled next to my ear as his grip tightened painfully. "You hear me?" I nodded, and he released me. "Now get in there and fix my dinner!"

I moved as quickly as my pregnant body would allow. I had taken out some pork chops earlier in the day, and quickly began to heat the oven. I knew that the night wasn't going to get better for me, but I didn't want it to get worse.

ooooOOOO

When I woke up the next morning, something seemed different. Warren was already out of bed. As I made my way downstairs, I could smell coffee. Warren never made coffee, at least not in years. I stepped into the kitchen to be met with someone who couldn't be my husband. He was standing in front of the stove, cooking eggs. "Good morning." He glanced at me over his shoulder and then went back to what he was doing.

"Good morning." My voice shook. Was this some kind of trick? Maybe I really was going crazy.

"There's coffee if you want some." He motioned to the coffee maker. I went to reach for a mug, and he stopped me. "Here." He handed it to me, and I jumped back. What was going on?

"Thanks," I whispered.

"I have a meeting this morning, but thought I'd fix us some breakfast first." He plated the eggs and carried them over to the table.

"Thanks." I slowly sat and stared at the plate. I was afraid to eat them. What if he did something to them? What if this was a trick?

"I know I don't cook much, but they can't be that bad." He shrugged as he scooped a giant bite into his mouth. I watched, wide-eyed, as he slowly chewed and swallowed. "If you don't want them, I'll eat them." He motioned to my untouched plate.

"Oh, I want them." I stared at my plate. "They were a little hot." I went with a logical excuse.

We sat there eating in silence as I wracked my brain for why he was doing this. Warren never did anything nice, and this had to mean something else. It couldn't just be breakfast.

"I have a business dinner scheduled for tonight. I was thinking I could just have it here." There it was, the catch. "I won't have to be out late this way."

"Ok," I mumbled. I knew I didn't have a choice. He wasn't asking, he was telling. By doing this, he was making sure I didn't leave the house today. It would take me all day to clean everything to his liking, and cook a meal that he approved of. The fact that he dirtied half the stuff in the kitchen to cook eggs insured that I'd be preparing all day.

"Sorry about all the mess." He smiled, but it wasn't a smile. It was a warning. "See you tonight." He wiped his mouth, tossed the napkin on the table, and left me there.

I surveyed the mess as I finished eating. There was a sink full of dishes, and several pots that were dirty. Dirt was tracked in on the floor as if he'd walked around the yard a few times first. The stove had splatters all over it. Warren knew how to pick up after himself, he just always chose not to. Honestly, it wouldn't bother me so much if I thought it was accidental, but this was done with purpose.

He put on the act of being nice just to draw me in. I let my guard down, and boom, he drops the hammer. By the time I'm ready for tonight, I won't even be able to enjoy it. I'll be exhausted, but he'll force me to smile and play the loving wife as he lies to his clients in our own house.

Today just might be the push that I need, the push to leave.

Chapter 4

Brooke

I've been scrubbing this house from top to bottom all day. I've had a ham cooking in the oven for most of the afternoon, and I've been hoping that this is good enough to get me through the night. Warren has always put on a show in front of our friends, but it's after it's all over that things change. The last time he had a business dinner, it ended with a beating. I only hope that this one is different.

It was around five when Warren came home. He was whistling when he stepped through the door. I knew that it was a warning. Whenever he wanted to appear relaxed, he would whistle. You could tell by the pitch if he was angry or satisfied with what he found. I was trying to change into something he'd find presentable, but my nerves held me captive. His heavy footsteps made it easy to tell where he was.

He ambled around the living room, then into the kitchen. I could hear the oven door open and close. His whistling made a sound of approval. He moved to the dining room, then I heard him on the stairs. As he climbed them, my heart raced and my muscles tightened. I stood in front of the full-length mirror, appraising myself. I still had a small bruise on my forehead, but other than that, I looked pretty normal. The soft cotton dress stretched across my belly before hanging loosely to the ground. It was a deep burgundy with a plunging neckline.

"Everyone will be here in an hour." Warren leaned his shoulder against the door frame to our bedroom.

"Ok." I nodded. "I'm ready."

"Good." It was all he said. He stared at me for a moment, and then walked away. No compliment, no 'thanks for getting everything ready', no anything. I don't know why I expected things to be different, I guess it just hurt that he didn't care.

oooooooo

Our guests arrived right when Warren said they would. He ushered them into the living room and offered everyone a drink. They sat and talked while I put the finishing touches on dinner. My back ached from bending over, and my feet were swollen from standing all day.

By the time I was bringing everything to the dining room, Warren and our guests were coming in to sit down. He thanked all of them for coming. "It makes things so much easier for us to have the meeting here. Brooke's pregnancy has been hard, and she needs to be able to rest more. It's easier on her to be home rather than in a stuffy restaurant." He smiled at me, and I nodded. I knew I needed to agree with him even though it was a line of bullshit. If they'd gone to a restaurant, he wouldn't have taken me. He'd have had me stay home and order take out. I never attended these events unless they were in our home.

"Everything smells and looks delicious." One of the gentlemen smiled at me.

"I can't believe you did all this, at seven months pregnant no less," another complimented.

"She does a lot," Warren grumbled slightly. I could tell it was killing him that they were being nice to me.

I spent most of the evening just sitting there trying not to yawn. Yawning meant boredom to Warren, and I wasn't allowed to be bored. The small group chatted about business and a few suggestions on which way the company should go. I wasn't really listening, and didn't care.

It was late when they left. I could barely keep my eyes open, but I knew I had to. Warren walked our guests to the front door to say his goodbyes. They waved to me, and thanked me for the delicious dinner before disappearing into the darkness.

I smiled before heading for the stairs. "Where are you going?" Warren demanded.

"To change." I motioned to my dress. It was a comfortable dress, but it was still a dress. I wanted to take off the heels and put on pjs and slippers.

"The dining room is a mess, and so is the kitchen." He pointed in the direction of the table that was still cluttered with dirty dishes.

"I can get that in a moment. I'd like to get comfortable first," I begged.

"You can get it now!" He stormed over to stand in front of me. "I expect messes to be cleaned after they're made, not later," he barked as he reached up and grabbed my hair right at the base of my head. "When I ask for something to be done, it needs to be done now, not later." He forced me to walk with him into the dining room. "Now, clean this up!" He all but tossed me towards the table before turning to storm out of the room. "I swear, I don't understand why you can't fucking listen to me," he grumbled as he walked away.

My shoulders shook as I attempted to hold back the tears. My feet ached, and as I slowly slipped the heels off, they sighed in relief. I wiped my forehead with the back of my hand as I stood, braced my back as I stretched, and then lifted a stack of plates to carry them into the kitchen. I flipped the water on before going back to the dining room. I wanted to make quick work of the mess, but knew it would take me at least an hour.

As I shuffled along, I let my mind wander. Could I really do this? What would my life be like trying to keep up with Warren's demands and a new baby?

"Brooke!?" his voice held a warning as he called from somewhere down the hallway, his office I assumed.

"Yes?" I tried to sound sweet as the bile rose in my throat. I knew deep down that he wasn't finished inflicting his pain for the night.

"We have to pay for water you know?" It was more of a growl now.

"I'm sorry. I needed it to warm up," I stammered. I didn't want to piss him off, but I was also mad. He wasn't going to help, but he was upset with my methods. What I wanted to say was, 'why don't you come help then?' but I knew that would only cause me more pain. "I'll turn it off," was all that came out.

I finished washing the dishes, wiped down the counters, and then began the trek upstairs. I flipped light switches off as I passed, and when I came to his office, I saw it was already dark. This could be good or bad. Warren may already be in bed, but if he wasn't asleep it could mean a long night for me.

I slowly climbed the stairs, stopping every few steps to rest. When I reached the top, I could see a light glowing in our room. My shoulders sagged with the realization that he was awake. So much for a quiet night. I lifted my chin as I stepped over the threshold.

"What took you so long?" he demanded as he rose from where he was perched on the edge of the bed.

"I'm sorry. The kitchen was a mess. It took me longer than I planned," I murmured as I shuffled over to the closet. I began to slip off my dress, but Warren had other plans.

"I've been waiting for you," he growled as he tugged at the material. "I have an early morning tomorrow, and you've kept me waiting long enough." The material slipped down my body as he rudely jerked it off.

"Can we not do this tonight? I'm really tired," I begged.

"Why are you tired? You're here all day laying around." His lips thinned as he glared at me. This was the Warren I was used to.

"I'm pregnant." I sighed. "The baby makes me tired." I whispered the words so quietly that I didn't think he heard them at first.

"The baby," he said like a statement before raising his voice. "The baby!" he bellowed. "This is the exact reason why I didn't want this thing!" He grabbed me by my shoulder and shoved me against the bed.

"Please!" I begged.

"Please what?" he screamed. "Don't fuck you?" I swear I saw fire shoot from his ears. "You're my wife. I'll do with you as I please!" He stormed closer, raising his fist.

It came at me with brute force, but I rolled to the side and lifted my arms for protection. The doctor had warned me that another blow to my head could cause permanent brain damage.

"When I feel like fucking you, I will!" he shouted as he grabbed my legs and attempted to pin me down. I don't know where it came from, but part of me snapped. I've never fought back. I've always just tried to convince him to stop while protecting myself. Tonight was different though. That part of you that comes alive when you become a parent came alive tonight.

"No!" I shouted back as I kicked my feet at him.

He looked at me with disbelief before jumping back into action. He grabbed a handful of hair and pulled me upright. My scalp stung as he forced me to walk around the room, heading straight for the door. My hands flew in front of my face on instinct; Warren's thrown me against the door before.

When we walked into the hallway, I began clawing at his grip. I needed him to let go, but he had no intention of doing so. He forced me over to the top of the stairwell, and paused. "This is your fault, you stupid whore. I never wanted this kid, and I intend to get rid of it."

Fear seized me as I twisted in his arms. His words felt like a thousand knives hitting me all at once. It was finally happening. He was gonna kill me. One hand moved from my hair to my back, and then in one fluid motion, he shoved me down the stairs.

I remember pain as I bounced against the wood. My arms instinctively went to my belly to protect my baby, leaving my head and back to take the brunt of the fall. I hit a few spindles on the way down before coming to rest on the tile floor of the hallway. His maniacal laugh sounded from above before my world went black once again.

Chapter 5

Blake

My night had started out like every other night. I was the on-call neurologist for the ER. It had been slow, so I'd gone outside to the ambulance bay to take a break. The air was crisp, and it felt like winter wasn't too far away.

When I heard the sirens in the distance, I knew the night was getting ready to get busy for someone, but I didn't expect it to be me. The lights flashed as the rig came to a halt a few feet away. "Dr. Douglas." The EMT nodded as he jumped out to race around to the back.

"What'd we got?" Dr. Evans, the Chief of Emergency Medicine, rushed past me to the stretcher being lowered from the rig.

"Female, twenty-eight, multiple contusions, possible skull fracture, twenty-eight weeks pregnant, BP one ten over seventy, heart rate seventy-four." The EMT rambled off the details as he and his partner rushed through the doors, and followed Dr. Evans into a room.

"I'm gonna need you on this!" Dr. Evans shouted in my direction. I jumped from where I was leaning against the wall, and rushed after them.

The ER had morphed right before my eyes. There was a lull before, but now it was bustling with medical staff. Nurses were running in and out of the room Dr. Evans had just gone into, and it took me a second to get my bearings.

"It's Brooke Ellis," Donna, one of my nurses, came rushing out. "She told me he did this, and I didn't believe her." Her voice was laced with fear and regret.

I nodded as instinct took over and feelings were pushed aside. "What'd we got?" I rounded the gurney and began checking her eyes. "Pupils are reactive. I need a head CT." I gave my orders to the nurse.

"We're waiting on OB. The baby's heart rate is falling," another nurse stated as she checked the fetal heart rate a second time. "This baby needs to come out if it's gonna survive; I'm paging Dr. McGee again." She rushed out of the room, and that's when Brooke's eyes fluttered open.

"Help me," she mumbled. "Please."

"We're gonna help," I reassured her. "We need to check on the baby."

"Save her." She reached for me as I stepped back to allow Dr. McGee in with the ultrasound. "Please save her."

"We're gonna do everything we can, Brooke." Dr. McGee was all business. She placed the wand of the ultrasound on Brooke's belly. "Brooke." She handed the wand over as she lifted the railing to the gurney. "We're going to take you upstairs now. We need to get the baby out. Your placenta has a tear in it, and it's slowly getting worse."

"But she's too young." She started to cry.

"She's a fighter, Brooke. Just like you." Dr. McGee started pushing the gurney as nurses unhooked monitors and draped the cords over the rails.

"As soon as we get her out of surgery, you'll get your CT." Dr. McGee left, leaving me there with my head spinning.

"Any word on how this happened?" I turned to the EMTs who were packing up to head back out.

"We found her in her underwear at the bottom of the stairs. Her husband said she fell. If you ask me, I think he pushed her." One of them shrugged.

"Why do you say that?" I gripped the back of my neck. I shouldn't be this invested, but I couldn't help it. There was something about her, that made me care more than I should.

"He didn't even want to come with us. He didn't seem worried at all that she might die, or that the baby might not survive. Who does that?" The other EMT's eyes widened.

ooooooooo

I stood there staring at the scan of Brooke's brain. There was swelling on the right side that would have to be monitored, but she was conscious. As long as the pressure didn't increase, the injury could be treated without surgery. I sighed as I headed to her room to give her the news.

"Mrs. Ellis." I knocked on the door as I slowly pushed it open.

"Mmm." Her head lolled to the side as her eyes fluttered.

"Your scan shows some swelling, but I think we can treat it with medication as long as things don't worsen."

"My baby," she mumbled. "Where's my baby?"

"I can check on that for you." I patted her hand before leaning out of the door and looking for a nurse. I saw Donna rounding the corner, and stopped her. "She's asking about the baby. Do we know anything yet?"

"Brooke. Your daughter's doing well for a twenty-eight weeker." She smiled as she brushed past me and into the room. "She's in the NICU. They're helping her breathe, but she's a fighter." She lowered herself onto the bed, and I knew I needed to give them some time.

oooooooooo

Brooke

Everything hurt. My head, my side, my stomach, but most of all my heart. I was still trying to wrap my head around the fact that Warren did this with every intent of killing our daughter. How could someone who was supposed to love me be so callous? Did he ever love me? I'd been asking myself that a lot lately, but I was having a hard time believing that the answer might be 'no'.

"Your daughter wasn't oxygenating enough, so she's on a ventilator. She's a fighter though, just like her mama." The nurse, Donna, smiled softly before glancing away at something. "Brooke? Did he do this to you?"

I nodded, and it hurt. "Yes." I grimaced. "He wanted to have sex, and I didn't, so he pushed me down the steps." A single tear slipped from my eyes. "I don't know what to do."

"He's never gonna hurt you again. I'm going to help you. I'm sorry I didn't believe you the last time." Donna squeezed my hand. "Do you want to see your daughter?"

"It hurts to move." I gasped as I attempted to sit up.

"If we can get you in a wheelchair, I'll take you to the NICU." She motioned to the door, and then pressed a few buttons on the bed to cause it to rise. After placing a pillow in my lap, she turned me where my legs hung off the side of the bed. "Hold the pillow against your stomach for support and lean on me." She braced my back as I stood, and slowly helped me sit in the chair. My head spun for a moment, but then the ache in my side came back.

"You've got a couple of cracked ribs, and C-sections hurt, but it's nothing that won't heal." She patted my shoulder and then turned to push me into the hallway. "Hey, Dr. Blake?" she called out as we passed the nurse's station. The doctor from before turned and forced a smile on his face.

"Yes, Donna." He placed a pen in his pocket and leaned against the counter.

"Can you call your brother for me? Brooke here, needs to talk to him." She began moving as he nodded and we rounded the corner.

"Who's his brother? A doctor for the baby?" I scrunched my brow and it caused my head to throb.

"His younger brother is a cop. He can get the paperwork started to get you away from your husband." She said it so matter of factly as we entered a room with gowns stacked by the door. "I'm gonna drape this over you. It's to keep everything sanitized in the NICU."

She wheeled me through the next set of doors, and I was faced with rows of incubators. There were beeps of all different speeds; some bassinets had signs, some didn't. Three nurses moved around with precision, checking each baby, and making notes. A young woman sat in a rocking chair in the corner, cuddling a baby to her chest. She was humming quietly as a man stood behind her. He looked so scared, but you could tell he was trying to hide it.

"Morning, Maggie." Donna waved. "We're here to see baby Ellis."

"She's right over here." She led the way to an incubator in the far corner. "She's been doing well so far, no apnea."

I stared at my daughter through the glass. She was covered in tubes and wires. She was so tiny, barely two pounds. Her little arms twitched every few seconds like she was searching for something. The cap on her head barely fit. There were these little fabric sunglasses covering her eyes, and the diaper was as big as she was.

"It looks worse than it is at the moment. She's a fighter." Maggie smiled softly as she opened one of the little portals. "Would you like to touch her?"

I needed this. I wanted to hold her, but we weren't there yet. I slowly lifted my arm. It felt like a lead weight was holding it down as I stretched it out and reached inside. I carefully touched her arm. She flinched, but then settled as I started talking to her.

"She knows your voice," Maggie encouraged.

My daughter settled as I told her I loved her, and then she wrapped her tiny fingers around mine. "She's holding on." I started to cry.

"She's your purpose," Donna whispered from behind me. It was like déjà vu. My world paused before starting to spin once again. I'd heard this before, but it wasn't here.

"You told me that the last time." I glanced at Donna. "That she was my purpose."

"She is," Donna reaffirmed. She didn't tell me I was wrong or question what I was talking about. She let me be right in this moment. "What's her name?"

"Ava," I whispered back. I let my thumb slide lightly over Ava's hand. "I love you." I sniffed as I leaned impossibly closer. "I'm gonna protect you, and you're going to have a great life." Her fingers twitched again, and I knew she understood me.

It was that moment that changed it all. I wasn't going to live in fear ever again. I was going to flourish on my own. I had a purpose, a reason to leave, and that purpose was her. I don't know how I'll do it, but I will. Today was the beginning, the beginning of a new life, a life away from pain and fear.

Chapter 6

Brooke

My days have been spent going from my room to the NICU. I spend as much time as I can with Ava, but I'm still healing myself. It's been three days since I arrived at the emergency room. Dr. Douglas, or Dr. Blake as the nurses call him, has been by every day to check my head. I've had several scans, and he says I'm healing well. I can't help but feel attached. He looks just like Officer Blake, but he doesn't act like him.

I've been able to sort more out in my head and determine what was real, and what wasn't. I still can't remember how I ended up in the hospital the first time, but Dr. Blake says it takes time to remember sometimes. Warren's been by once, but security stopped him. I decided to press charges, so a police officer is supposed to be coming by later to take my statement. Donna says it's a long process, but she'll stay with me as long as I want.

"Mrs. Ellis?" I looked up to see a man in a suit knocking on the doorway to my room. "I'm Detective Douglas. I'm here to take your statement." He smiled softly and I could see the family resemblance.

"You're Dr. Blake's brother." I smiled back. It was the first time I'd smiled in a long time.

"Yes." He chuckled. "I hope he hasn't been talking about me too much. Mind if I come in?"

"Sure." I pushed a few buttons to make the bed sit up a little straighter. I was still pretty sore, but I'd been getting up and walking since last night.

"You can call me Cal." He held out his hand for me to shake.

"Ok, Cal." I nodded as I shifted on the bed. I wasn't sure what I was supposed to do. "What's next?"

"Well, the first thing we're going to do is press charges for battery. We can't really prove that he was trying to kill you, but he was trying to hurt you. The most important thing that you need to remember is, we're on your side. He may try to intimidate you once we move forward, but you need to stay your ground. We're going to use this as evidence when we file the order of protection. The fact that this fall caused you to have to deliver early, and the baby was premature is going to work in our favor. I've got reports from your doctor, the emergency room staff, and the nurses in the NICU. I have a good feeling that you'll be granted the order."

"How am I going to keep him away?" I twisted the sheets in my hand.

"Once the order is granted, he'll be served. If he doesn't comply, he can be arrested. If he breaks the order, you call the police." Cal jotted a few things down on a piece of paper before looking back over at me. "Do you have a place to go when you're discharged? A family member or friend's house?"

"No. Warren made sure I didn't have any friends, and my parents died years ago. I'm an only child." I shook my head as I looked away. "He picked me because of that, didn't he? I'm weak," I growled.

"You're not weak. He is." Cal's eyes were sad as he watched me. "Men like him are the weak ones, that's why they beat women. It makes them feel powerful."

"I should have left a long time ago." I punched the mattress beside me.

"You're leaving now. That's what matters. Here," he handed me a card, "this is the number for a local women's shelter. They take women and children. They'll help you get back on your feet until you find a place to live on your own."

"I don't know how to thank you." I took the paper and squeezed it in my hand.

"Survive. That's thanks enough." He smiled. "I'm going to get a few more things from your doctors and then I'm going to head over to drop it all off with the DA. You should have that protection order by tomorrow night."

"Thanks, Cal." I waved as he left. It was the first time I ever felt like someone was really on my side. He believed me, and offered me support. I hadn't had that in a man since I was little and my dad helped me.

ooooooooo

I spent most of the afternoon and all of that night in the NICU. Ava was still doing well, but I missed being with her. I was going to be discharged the next day, but Ava had to stay. She'd be here for at least four more weeks. She had to gain weight, and start eating before she could leave.

"You wanna hold her?" Maggie smiled as she opened the door on the side of the incubator.

"Can I?" I was hopeful. I'd been bonding with my daughter solely on touches and talking.

"She's been breathing on her own; you just need to be careful with supporting her head. Skin to skin contact helps preemies." I watched as Maggie lifted Ava from the incubator. She turned in my direction, and I sat in a nearby rocker. I tugged my gown out the way, and Maggie placed Ava against my chest. "Just support her head," she whispered as she removed her hands.

I leaned back in the rocker as my tiny daughter stayed cuddled against my chest. She was so little, barely the size of a small doll. The breathing tube had been replaced by a smaller oxygen tube. She still had some wires monitoring her heart rate and other bodily functions, but for the most part we were almost normal. She'd gained a few ounces over the last week, and I was hopeful she'd be moved out of the NICU in the next week.

"We've been offering her bottles, but she gets too tired to suck. I don't think it'll be long though." Maggie wrote some things down on Ava's chart and then started to walk away. "Let me know when you're ready to put her back, and I'll come help you."

"Thanks." I gently caressed Ava's head. "It'll be a while I'm sure." I'd hold my daughter all the time if I could. The fear of falling asleep and dropping her was ever present though.

oooooooooo

It's been two days, and I'm sitting on the edge of my bed holding on to a stack of discharge papers. Dr. Blake cleared me to leave this morning, and Dr. McGee cleared me last night. I've been down to tell Ava that I'll see her tomorrow, and now I'm waiting for the orderly to come wheel me downstairs. Dr. Blake offered to have a cab called for me and it should be here in the next few minutes.

"Ready to go." A young man stopped in the doorway with a wheelchair.

"I guess." I wasn't real keen on leaving. Leaving meant I had to deal with Warren. I wouldn't have the hospital staff intervening for me anymore, and it also meant that Ava and I wouldn't be so close to each other. Leaving also meant that I could start to move on, which was a good thing. I needed to break free and do what I wanted. I needed to start my life over, and not have to worry about Warren during every step I took.

I lowered myself into the wheelchair, and let the orderly push me down to the front doors to leave. A yellow cab was waiting when we got there. "Thanks." I stood, and grabbed the small bag containing the few items I had at the hospital. I climbed into the cab, clutching the paper that Cal had given me. It was my destination until I could figure things out. A safe place, a place to make a plan for Ava's and my future.

"Good luck." The orderly waved as I closed the cab's door and pulled away from the curb.

Things looked different this time as I rode through the city. The fall colors seemed brighter, the sky bluer, the air felt crisper. It was as if I was seeing and feeling everything for the first time. That weight that I always carried around was gone, and even though I was scared of what was to come, I knew it had to be better than what I was leaving behind.

oooooooooo

The cab stopped in front of a gray stone house not far from where I lived with Warren. It looked like any other house on the block. Mums were growing in pots that lined the stairs leading to the front porch, a wreath made of fall leaves hung on the door, and the lawn was neatly mowed.

"This is it, ma'am." The cabbie glanced back at me. "Fare was already paid by a doctor."

"Oh, ok," I stuttered as I opened the door. While I was climbing out, a young woman came out onto the porch. She smiled and waved at me. "Thanks." I closed the door, and the cab left.

"Hi. I'm Amy." She jogged down the steps. "You must be Brooke."

"Yes." I slowly climbed the steps. I still ached slightly and movement hurt.

"Donna said you'd be coming today. Let me help you." She wrapped her arm around my back and helped me up the steps. "We're all happy you're here, and anything you need, just ask."

"We?" I glanced around. I didn't see a bunch of people.

"Most of us work during the day. I had the day off. Donna usually gets here in the evening unless she has the night shift. You know Donna. She said she was your nurse." Amy opened the door and stepped back to let me in.

"Donna lives here?" I was confused.

"Yeah. She runs this place. She works at the hospital to make money to keep it running. We get donations, but it's not always enough, ya know?" She shrugged. "I'll show you your room if you follow me." She waved and started walking down a long hallway. "This is you. Donna put a crib in here for when your baby comes."

I stepped through the door and looked around. It was simple. A twin bed on one wall, a small dresser, and a chair in the corner.

"I know it's not much, but you can always add things. You're fortunate Margaret just moved out last week, otherwise we wouldn't have had space." Amy chattered on. "If your husband shows up here, lock the door and call the police. There's a phone in every room. In order to comply with the order of protection, he can't be on our property if you are."

"I don't think Warren will care. He didn't want the baby," I mumbled.

"Maybe not, but you'd be surprised what some of these men do when they see they can't control you. Most of them don't care, they just want the control. When you take that away, they turn even worse. Does your husband own a gun?" Amy's eyes looked fearful.

"I don't know. He kept me in the dark about a lot of things. He liked keeping me on edge." I sighed.

"That's the control. Just make sure you call the police if he shows up." Her face was stern.

"Won't someone be here?" I stammered.

"Maybe. It depends on everyone's schedule. We all have jobs. We all work different hours, but sometimes you might be here alone. Donna will help you find a job, so you'll need to come up with a plan for that too. You need to plan out what you're going to do if you see him public."

"I didn't think of that," I muttered as I stared at my feet. This seemed like so much work.

"I know it's overwhelming, but you'll see. This is the first step to independence. In a month, you won't even remember this version of yourself." Amy smiled as she backed out of the room. "I'll let you have some time to yourself. Dinner is at six, if you want to eat with us. If you don't, there's always leftovers in the fridge. Just heat up what you want." She turned to head down the hallway, leaving me there in the room.

"Oh, Brooke," she stuck her head back around the doorway, "welcome home. I'm glad you're here." She smiled and then disappeared again.

I was glad to be home too. Just knowing that I could eat dinner when I wanted was a satisfactory feeling. I could start to do things my way, and that little ember in my soul started to glow. I would feed that ember, and soon my flame would burn bright once again. Warren wouldn't snuff me out anymore.

Chapter 7

Brooke

Over the next week my schedule was pretty much the same. I'd wake up, take a cab to the hospital, and spend the day in the NICU with Ava. She was doing great, much better than some of the other babies. There was one day that I was afraid to leave. They had a baby stop breathing and called a code. It was one of the scariest things I've ever witnessed. The parents stood there, helpless, as they watched the nurses and doctors swarm the incubator. After a few minutes the baby started breathing again and things calmed down. Maggie explained that sometimes that happens with preemies, they just forget to breathe.

Today was going to be different though. Today I was going back to Warren's house to get my things. Cal had stopped by yesterday to let me know that Warren had been served the order of protection papers, and I should get my things. I was entitled to them. He suggested going by when Warren would be in the office, but also said he could come and escort me. I figured that was a good idea since I wasn't really sure of what hours Warren was keeping at the office. The order of protection wouldn't help me if I came to him.

"Brooke." Cal smiled when he climbed out of a dark sedan. The passenger side door opened and Dr. Blake climbed out too.

"Hi." My brow scrunched. I was confused.

"Cal thought you might need some help. Today's my day off," Dr. Blake clarified.

"Thanks, Dr. Blake." I moved closer to the car.

"You can call me Blake." He smiled. "My friends don't use the doctor part."

"We don't?" Cal sounded amused.

"You're family, not a friend." Blake shot a warning glare.

"Ouch!" Cal placed his hand over his chest. "Let's get going. I really don't want to arrest anyone today." Cal climbed back in just as I reached the car.

ooooooooo

"Thanks for doing this," I murmured as we climbed the steps to the brownstone. I hadn't been here since the night Warren pushed me down the steps.

"No problem." Blake smiled. "How are we getting in?" He glanced at Cal.

"There's a hide a key out here." I reached for the little frog that was sitting by the door, produced the key that was hidden in his belly, and slipped into the lock, but the lock wouldn't budge.

"What's wrong?" Cal stepped closer and attempted to turn the key.

"It won't open," I grunted.

"That jackass changed the locks," Blake grumbled.

"Hang on." Cal rolled his eyes before going back to his car. A moment later, he jogged up the steps carrying a small black case.

"What's that?" I pointed at his hands.

"Our way in." Cal smiled as he opened the case and produced several small screwdrivers. "I knew this would come in handy one day." He slipped the tools into the lock and went to work picking it. Within a few seconds, the door slipped open.

"Nice." Blake nodded as Cal stepped back and let us pass.

"What happens if he finds out you did this?" I turned worried eyes on them both.

"This is still your house. You have as much right to be here as he does. You gave me permission to get in. He can't do anything." Cal shrugged. "Get your things while I keep watch." He pointed into the house. I moved as fast as my body would allow as I shuffled toward the stairs. The scene I was met with made me skid to a halt.

There on the floor was a blood stain along with another broken spindle. "What the hell?" Blake gasped from behind me.

"This is his doing. He did this last time. He left the mess for me to clean," I grumbled as I carefully stepped around the destruction. I shook my head as I climbed the stairs to our room. This would be the last time I entered this hell hole.

I wandered inside our bedroom, and turned toward the closet. I didn't even want to look at the bed. The dress I'd worn to dinner that night was still crumpled in a pile on the floor. Flashes of that evening assaulted me. I could feel his hands on my body as I grabbed clothes from the closet. I could hear his voice right beside my ear as I tossed them on the bed. Him grabbing my hair and dragging me to the top of the steps played like a movie in my head.

I yanked piece after piece of clothing off the hanger. I tossed shoes on the bed with them. I grabbed things from my dresser, piling them on too. Anger boiled out of me as I stomped around the room. I could do this my way. He wasn't here to critique me.

"You ok?" Blake's voice was quiet as he stood by the door, watching.

"I'm fine," I snapped. "Just dealing with ghosts is all."

"Do you need help?" He stepped forward.

"Yes. Grab the edge of the comforter over there. I'm taking this." I balled up the purple and gold comforter from our bed, the comforter that Warren complained about all the time. I used it as a sack of sorts to carry my things. Blake carried the bundle downstairs and I followed. I took every piece of clothing that was mine except the burgundy dress. I left it in the bottom of the closet as a reminder for Warren. He could pick it up. He could have it. It was the final straw. It symbolized me leaving, and I wanted him to think about the fact that it was his fault every time he saw that dress. I wanted him to remember that all of this was his fault.

oooooooooo

Blake

I've never met a woman as strong as Brooke. The pure determination on her face as we carried her belongings out to my brother's cruiser was a sight to behold. Her husband was a real piece of work, and I truly don't understand how she lived with him for as long as she did.

I stuffed the homemade sack into the trunk and then turned to see her standing on the bottom step. "You ready?"

"Almost," she grumbled. "I just need a minute."

"It's ok to not be ok today. You know that, right?" I stepped up behind her.

"I do." She nodded. "I just need to remember how bad he was. I need to keep all of that fresh so I can fight him. Warren won't go away without a fight. He's not wired that way." Her voice sounded sad, defeated almost.

"You can do this. I'll help you do this." I don't know where those words were coming from. I didn't really know her other than the fact that she was my patient, and she wasn't even really that anymore.

"Let's get out of here," Cal called from the top of the steps. He was just starting to lock the door when Brooke stopped him.

"Leave it unlocked." She smirked. "I want him to worry for a few seconds before he figures out it was me."

I almost laughed in that moment. She didn't look like the scared woman I'd seen several months ago. At this moment in time, she looked as if she was finally taking a piece of her life back.

"Sure." Cal shrugged as he jogged toward the car. "I wish I could be here when he shows up."

"No, you don't," Brooke muttered as she climbed in the car. "No one wants to be here when he shows up. I've seen him blow up more times than I can count, and this blow will be on a scale of Chernobyl."

ooooooooo

Brooke

It didn't take us long to get back to the house. Amy was sitting on the front porch reading when we pulled up. She waved as I climbed out, and I realized that this house truly felt like a home should. It was the first time that I believed I'd be ok. Bringing Ava here didn't scare me, and I didn't have that churning in my gut that I got every time I went to the brownstone. This place felt the way I should have felt for years. This place was the new beginning I'd been searching for.

"Everything go ok?" Amy jogged down the steps.

"Yep." I moved away from the car as Blake grabbed my sack from the trunk.

"You don't own any luggage?" Amy laughed.

"I do, but leaving the bed in an unorganized mess is much more satisfying." I lifted my chin in the small amount of pride I was starting to feel. Donna had told me to always be on the lookout, but in this moment, I wanted to celebrate. 'Celebrate the small stuff', she'd said.

"Where are we taking this?" Blake hoisted the bundle over his shoulders.

"The second door on the left." I pointed down the hallway to the room I'd been staying in. As Blake walked away, I turned to Cal. "I can't thank you enough for everything you've done to help. I don't know how I'll ever repay you."

"Survive." Cal smiled. "Love your daughter. Teach her what a good man is. Be happy. Be successful. Love with all your heart."

"Those are things that'll help me." I was confused.

"Yes, but it means I was successful if you are successful." He held out his hand to shake. I took it, and he shook my hand softly as a smile tugged at his lips. I couldn't help but turn away. I'd never had a man look at me like that, not even Warren.

"Ready?" Blake cleared his throat and Cal looked over my shoulder at him.

"Sure." Cal laughed lightly and then turned to leave. "Bye, Brooke. If you need anything, you know where to reach me." He waved, and then climbed into his car.

I stood there, waiting for Blake to wave, but he didn't. He barely glanced in my direction as they pulled away from the curb. It was as if he was mad. I knew the signs from watching Warren all those years, but I didn't understand what he could possibly be upset about. We were successful today, and I thanked him. I stayed rooted in place over thinking everything, because that's what I did. My head started to ache, so I moved to the porch swing. I played the events of the day over and over in my head as I tried to figure out how I upset him. It had to be my fault. These things were always my fault. Warren made sure I understood that. I'd made Blake mad, and I had to figure out why.

Chapter 8

Brooke

A month has passed since I moved into Donna's place which I learned was called Emily's House. There's a story behind that name, but it's not a nice one. Emily was the first woman Donna tried to help. She went back to her husband, and he ended up killing her. Donna said she swore it would never happen again. Since opening Emily's House, Donna's saved over fifty women, and helped them get back on their feet. She's helped them find jobs, and courage to make it on their own. I'm the only resident without a job, but Donna says she's got a few ideas to help me. I'm supposed to be meeting with her tomorrow because today is a big day. In just a few hours I'll be on my way to the hospital to pick up Ava. She's coming home today, and I can't wait.

Donna and I went to the local Rescue Mission and with donations to the House, we've been able to buy other things that I needed. I was able to get assistance through the government, but Warren has already challenged that. He claimed that I was still a dependent, and he was planning to add the baby as a dependent too. I hired a divorce lawyer who's taking my case pro bono. She said I had a better chance of getting support for Ava if I let Warren claim her. I don't know how I feel about that, but with Warren having a steady job it will be easier to enforce child support. I just don't want him to get visitation. After what he put me through and threatened to do to her, I can't imagine what visits would be like.

"You about ready?" Donna leaned in through the doorway.

"Ready for what?" I was confused. Donna was supposed to be at work. "I thought you were at the hospital all day today."

"I had someone cover the afternoon for me. I thought you might want a ride to the hospital. This way you don't have to bring Ava home in a cab." Donna smiled.

"That would be great." I couldn't help it, tears started to leak from my eyes.

"Don't cry on me, now," Donna tsked. "Today is supposed to be a happy day."

"It is. These are happy tears. I've just never had anyone who cared about me like you do; not since my parents anyway." I wiped at my eyes. Things had been so different since I moved in. I was making friends with the other women, I was learning to open up more in therapy, and now Ava was coming home.

"All right. Well, grab the car seat, and let's head out. I'm sure the NICU nurses will want to go over everything before you leave." Donna led the way out to her car parked on the street. I placed the car seat in the backseat before climbing into the front.

oooooooooo

It didn't take us long to arrive at the hospital. Donna let me out by the front door, and promised to meet me upstairs after she parked. I lugged the car seat along as I headed toward the elevators. When I reached them, I set the car seat on the ground and pushed the call button.

"They've been really slow all day. Might take a while." A male voice sounded from behind me.

I turned around to see Blake breezing down the hallway in his white lab coat. "What are you doing over here?" I scrunch my brow. Neurology was several floors up.

"I heard you were picking up Ava today. I thought I'd take a chance that you might be arriving soon." He shrugged as a smile pulled at his lips.

"You came to see Ava?" I was surprised, shocked almost.

"And you." His lip curled as a shy smile appeared. "Hope that's ok."

"Sure." It was that moment that the elevator dinged and the doors opened in front of us. I lifted the car seat with a heavy sigh.

"Let me help." Blake grabbed the handle from me, causing our hands to brush together. I could tell he noticed because his body went kinda stiff.

"Thanks." I released where I was holding and stepped into the elevator. I'd been making this trip for the last four weeks, but today would be different; I wasn't leaving alone.

"No problem. These things weigh a ton." He laughed lightly to break the tension before following me into the elevator.

As the doors closed and we began rising, the tension began to come back. "So, why Ava?" I turned slightly, but didn't face him directly. "I mean, I'm your patient and I'm fine now."

"Yes, that's true, but I've read a few of Ava's scans too." Blake stumbled over his words almost.

"Oh." The doors opened and when we stepped off, Donna was leaning against the wall across from us. "Wait?! How did you beat me?"

"My parking spot is on this level. I used the walkway and just came across." She smiled. "Dr. Blake." She nodded at him with a knowing look and he blushed. I'd never seen a man blush before, but Donna had quite the effect on Blake.

"Afternoon, Donna." He nodded as he motioned for us to lead the way to the entrance of the NICU.

As I stood there listening to all the instructions from the nurses for Ava, Donna and Blake stood in the background. "I think I'll be fine," I told Maggie. "I'm staying with Donna, so she can help me if I need it." Maggie gave me a bag filled with diapers and formula samples. It was enough for a few days until I was able to get to the store. She helped me buckle Ava in, and then watched as the three of us walked out the door.

"I can carry that if you'd like." Blake motioned to the carrier in my arms.

"It is heavy, but I want to do it." I struggled. "I need to do things for myself. I know you're trying to help, but you won't be there all the time." I sighed as we headed for the walk thru that Donna had taken.

"Oh, right," Blake mumbled. "Let me give you my number here in case you have any questions. I don't live far from where you're staying. I can drop by after shift if you ever need anything."

"Um, ok." I was caught off guard. Blake was acting weird. It was like he didn't want me to go, but had no reason to make me stay.

He stuffed a business card in my hand, "Anytime, night or day, and I'll answer." He waved before heading back to the elevator bank.

"What has gotten into Dr. Blake?" Donna shook her head as we reached the walk thru.

"That was weird, right? It wasn't just me?" I stuffed the card in my pocket as we went into the parking garage.

"He was tongue tied like a school boy." She laughed. "I think he might like you."

"No." I shook my head.

"We'll soon find out," she teased.

"What do you mean by that?" I lifted the car seat into the back of her car. It snapped into place, and I closed the door.

"If I'm right, he'll find a way to come by the house. He already helped you move out, and then today he showed up for this. I know your radar is all kinds of messed up from your ex, but Dr. Blake's signals are there." She laughed as she climbed in the car.

Was I that blind, or was Donna seeing things that just weren't there? I thought about this the entire ride home. Ava was quiet in the back, and Donna was humming to herself. It had been a long time since a man showed interest in me. Warren had trained me to ignore it. If we were ever out and a man was so much as polite to me, Warren would punish me when we came home. He was constantly accusing me of cheating. I never so much as looked at another man, but that didn't matter. In his eyes, I was asking for it.

When we arrived home, Donna helped me carry Ava's things into my room. I placed the carrier on my bed and lifted Ava out to cuddle with her. Before placing her in the crib, I wanted to spend time with her. Donna must have noticed this because she quietly slipped out the door to give us some time.

I laid on the bed with Ava beside me, just caressing her soft hair. She was sound asleep and didn't even flinch when I shifted, causing the mattress to bounce slightly. Ava stretched and yawned after a few minutes, blinking up at me. "Hey baby," I cooed. "Mommy is so happy to have you home."

Ava's mouth opened as if she was going to say something, but then closed again. She blinked a few times more before lifting her fist to her lips. As soon as she found her mouth, she began sucking. "Are you hungry?" I searched the room, finding the bottles we'd brought home sitting on my dresser.

I prepared one, and began feeding her as Donna's words tumbled around in my head. Was Blake really interested? How did that even work? I was still married, and wasn't sure I'd ever want to be involved with a man again. The only relationship I knew was a bad one, and I needed to concentrate on me. That was one of the few things that really stuck with me from therapy. I needed to worry about Ava and myself. The rest wasn't important at the moment. Once I got myself and my daughter taken care of, then I could look into other things. If Blake started coming around, I'd have to tell him that. I needed to concentrate on me.

Chapter 9

Brooke

"What do you think?" Donna swept her arm across the room. After I'd laid Ava down for an afternoon nap, Donna had asked me to come into her office.

"What do you mean, exactly?" I tipped my head to the side as I watched her, now more confused than ever.

"I really need someone here to answer phones and manage things when I'm at the hospital. I know this isn't what you went to college for, but I was thinking that you could do it for a while since Ava is so little still. We could bring the play yard in here for when you need to be here." Donna smiled and nodded.

"You mean work for you?" My brow crinkled. "Like here?" I pointed at the small desk in the corner.

"Yeah." She nodded again. "You can do this until next fall, then we'll try to get you into a school. Ava will be old enough then that it won't be so hard to leave her with a sitter. You may even be living on your own by that point."

I swallowed, "On my own?"

"Relax," she soothed. "I'm not kicking you out. You can stay as long as you need to, but I think you'll be ready then."

"Ok." I forced a smile. The idea of moving out scared the crap outta me. I'd just gotten settled here, and was in no hurry to leave.

"I'm off tomorrow, and then I work the night shift for two days. I can show you what to do, and the girls are in and out every day. Someone seems to always be here." Donna patted my arm. "Besides, I'm sure you'll have a visitor or two." She winked at me.

"What's that supposed to mean?" I clasped my hands in front of me.

"Dr. Blake seems to have taken a liking to you, and from what Amy said, so has his brother." She laughed and I couldn't help but turn away slightly. I could feel my face heating with embarrassment.

"I don't know about that," I muttered.

"Hey, I wouldn't mind attention from either one of them. They are both F-I-N-E, fine looking men." Donna grinned and my heart raced. Did I want attention from either of them? What if they hid things the way Warren did from his colleagues? What if they were different behind closed doors?

ooooooooo

It took about a week to get a time to meet but my lawyer, Veronica Ortiz, is meeting me at her office this afternoon. Donna is going to watch Ava and I'm signing the paperwork to get my divorce started.

Cal has been by a few times letting me know that the state is prosecuting Warren for criminal charges. Since the last incident involved Warren wanting to force me to have sex, the state is charging him with rape and sexual offense. If he's convicted, he won't be able to get custody of Ava.

Ava is an entirely different matter. Warren hasn't tried to claim custody, he hasn't come to see her, or attempted to contact me. I'm hoping to file abandonment charges against him for her. My lawyer says that since he's made no attempts to claim his rights, I have a pretty good chance of getting full custody with no visitation. As much as I would love for Ava to have a dad, I want her dad to be one who wants and loves her.

It only took me about twenty minutes to get to Roni's office. Emily's House is downtown as well as the building that houses Veronica's firm. I pulled my coat tighter around me as I stood there looking up at the dark glass structure. Winter was just beginning and it smelled as if snow was right around the corner.

I rode the elevator up to the seventeenth floor, staring through the glass the entire way. The sky was a dull gray, all the colorful leaves gone, leaving the trees bare. People were bustling about on the sidewalks, making them look like little ants from my view. When the doors opened, I stepped out into a luxurious office. Plush leather couches lined the waiting area. A large wooden desk sat off to the side with a young woman typing away on a computer behind it.

"Roni will be right out." She glanced up at me, not even stopping what she was working on.

"Thanks." I pulled my gloves off and stuffed them into my pockets.

"Brooke! Hi!" Veronica, Roni, smiled as she burst through the door. Her dark hair was pulled back in a low pony, and she was dressed in a navy pinstriped suit. "Sorry to keep you waiting," she called over her shoulder as she led me to an office near the end of the hallway.

"It's ok. I haven't been waiting long." I smiled as she stepped out of the way and let me pass. Once inside, I removed my coat and hat, and lowered myself onto the red leather chair in front of her desk.

"I've drawn up the paperwork to get things started here. A lot will depend on the criminal case. If your husband is found guilty, then it's going to be a slam dunk for us. I honestly don't know why he wouldn't, but you never can tell with some of these juries." She opened a manila folder stacked with papers in front of me. Tiny black print filled the pages. Some of it I understood, but there was a bunch of legal jargon too.

"Sign here," she pointed to the bottom of the second page, "here, here, and initial here, here, and here." She tagged each spot with a small red arrow sticker.

"That's it?" I sat back, slightly surprised that it wasn't harder than that.

"For you, yes. I'm sure I'll be going back and forth with his lawyer, but I've included everything you asked." She smiled as she straightened the papers.

"Even the custody agreement?" I was skeptical.

"Yes, although I can't promise anything on that one. The fact that he contested your application for assistance says he's going to contest this. I'm working on the child support application for you too."

"Thanks." I sighed. I was just ready for all of this to be over. Why would a man who so obviously hates me want to drag this out?

"I know this is hard. I've seen some men who just sign and get it over with, and I've seen some drag it out for years. I'm hoping that the criminal charges stick. You aren't seeing anyone, right?" Roni tapped her pen against her desk.

"No." I shook my head. "I've been too busy healing and taking care of my daughter. Besides, I don't think I could trust a man after what Warren did."

"If you do start seeing someone, I wouldn't broadcast it to your ex. He can make things a lot harder if he wants to. Jealous men don't think with their heads too well." She rolled her eyes before jotting down something on a card. "This is the case number for the criminal charges. You can check the progress by calling the station and asking for the detective in charge. Give them this case number and tell them you want updates."

"Thanks. I don't know how to thank you for this. I'd never be able to afford someone like you." I clutched the card in my hand.

"Donna's a good friend. She's helped a lot of people over the years, including my sister. She wasn't so lucky." Roni smiled sadly. "Emily was everything to me, that's why I've always helped women like her. My only payment is that you promise not to ever go back to him."

"I won't. Promise." As I stood up to put my coat back on, I saw several framed photos of Roni with another woman who looked just like her. Donna was in one of the photos. This was the Emily the house was named after. This was the Emily who started it all.

"Good." Roni jerked her head quickly. "I've got to get these to a courier so they can be served in the next few days. Don't go anywhere alone. Once he gets these, he may break the order of protection."

"I won't," I reiterated as I left her office. I walked back to the elevators with a little bounce in my step. Even though I still had a long way to go, I felt like I was finally doing something about it. Too many times I felt helpless when it came to Warren. It felt good to have friends and people who listened to me and wanted to help.

On the ride down, I stared at the card in my hand. I rubbed my gloved fingers over the lettering of my case number. I wasn't paying attention to my surroundings, and it cost me. When I stepped outside the building and onto the sidewalk, I glanced across the street. There, standing like a commanding statue, was Warren. He was dressed in a gray suit with a black overcoat. His briefcase was dangling from his left hand as a cell phone hung in his right. His eyes stared daggers right through me. I swallowed as I stumbled back slightly and he smirked, his mouth almost an evil grin.

Panic began to seize me. I turned, almost plowing into another bystander as I raced for the doors of the coffee shop next door. I looked back over my shoulder to see Warren still staring. He must have known that he couldn't come any closer, but it didn't stop him from trying to intimidate me from where he was.

I threw open doors to It's Latte and barreled inside, crashing right into someone, a very tall someone.

"Whoa," a male voice sounded as two strong hands grabbed my shoulders to steady me.

"Let go!" I yelled as I yanked back, almost falling backwards and back out the door.

"Brooke? Are you ok?" I looked up to see the blue eyes of Cal staring back at me.

"Cal. He's out there." I pointed at the door. "Warren's out there." Cal rushed outside, coffee in hand and stood on the sidewalk. I watched as he scanned the area before coming back in.

"He's gone now." He sighed. "Did he try to talk to you or get close?"

"No, he just stared." My voice shook as my heart thundered in my chest.

"Unfortunately, there's nothing I can do about that. As long as he stays a hundred feet away, he's within his rights."

"I'm just ready for this to all be over," I mumbled.

"I know, and it will be, it just might take a while." Cal nodded. "Hey, I was meeting someone here for coffee; want to join us?"

"I really can't. I need to get back to the house. Thanks." I waved as I turned toward the door. Roni's words of 'don't get involved with someone' ran through my head on a loudspeaker. I wasn't ready, but I couldn't chance it either.

"Suit yourself." He shrugged before waving to someone coming in. "S'up, Bro?"

I turned to see Blake glance up at us. His smile dropped and was immediately replaced by a frown. "I'll take mine to go," he grumbled as the barista handed Cal two cups. Cal's brow furrowed as Blake turned and left as quickly as he appeared.

I used that moment to escape too. I couldn't figure Blake out with his hot and cold moments. He seemed to want to be around me one day, and the next it was like I had the plague. My entire walk home was spent trying to figure why I made him mad. What did I do? Was Warren right? Was I just too stupid to see it?

Chapter 10

Blake

It's been a long day today, and all I can think about is getting home, having a beer, and relaxing. My brother has been getting on my last nerve the last few days, so like the mature person I am, I've been avoiding him. Guess he figured it out because just as I looked up, I saw him heading straight for me.

"Hey." Cal stopped at the nurse's station where I was currently filling out orders for a patient I'd just seen.

"Need something?" I muttered as I placed the file back on the counter. Donna smiled and nodded. I could tell that she was up to something, but I didn't know what at the moment. She'd been acting strange all day.

"I was hoping to grab a beer with you after shift, but you seem to be avoiding my calls." Cal shrugged as he leaned his hip against the counter.

"I've been busy," I grumbled as I started to walk away.

"Doing what?" Cal followed me. I don't know what his game is today. Shouldn't he be hanging out with Brooke? He's been with her the last few times I've seen him.

"Working." I shot him a warning glare. "Kinda like I'm trying to do right now?!" I stopped outside a patient's door. "Why don't you invite Brooke out with you? You seem to be pretty close now."

"What?" He shook his head. "I'm helping her with her case. Why does this bother you so much?" His brow furrowed and then his lips formed a giant smile. "Oh, I see." He chuckled. "You're jealous." He pointed at me and started laughing. "Dude, she's nice and all but we're just friends. You should ask her out if you like her."

"She's still married," I growled.

"Not for long. She filed the papers two weeks ago." He crossed his arms over his chest.

My eyes swung to his, "and you know this how?"

"She told me." He shrugged. "Probably would have told you too if you stuck around one of those times you've seen us."

I sighed. Cal was right. Every time I've seen them around town, I've rushed away in the other direction. Brooke had a horrible experience and I feel like I should leave her alone if she wants my brother. "I guess we can grab a beer later, but I have to get back to work." I pointed at the door of the room I was waiting to enter.

"I'll meet you at Bottom's Up around seven. Does that work?" Cal started to back up.

"Sure." I waved to him before entering the room. I really needed to finish my rounds if I wanted to have a chance of getting out of here on time.

oooooooOO

"Dr. Blake?" I'd just seen my last patient for the day and of course Donna picks now to tell me whatever's been going on.

"Yes." I sighed as I leaned against the nurse's station. I needed to look annoyed, but I was actually a little amused.

"You know, Thanksgiving is coming up in a week." Donna smiled but I could tell there was more here.

"Un huh." I nodded.

"Well, we always cook a big meal at the house and we never eat it all. I was wondering if you were off that day." She grinned even bigger.

"I actually am." I shifted on my feet. We rotate holidays here, and it was my year to have this one off.

"I was thinking maybe you could join us. I'm sure Brooke would be pleased." She leaned over on the counter as if she was sharing something with a girlfriend.

"Why do you say that?" I mused. It seemed like Donna was trying to play matchmaker, but I didn't think she'd be that obvious or devious.

"I have my ways." She tipped her head. "So, what'd ya say. Lunch? Around two?"

"I will do my best." I laughed. "Now you just need to keep something bad from happening and calling me in here," I joked as I handed off the last of the patient files, and turned to leave.

"Where you off to tonight?" Donna called out.

"Drinks with my brother." I waved without turning around.

"Invite him for Thanksgiving too. The more the merrier," she yelled, causing my shoulders to slump. Why oh why did my brother have to be included in this too?

oooooooooo

Brooke

It's been pretty quiet the last few weeks. I've only left the house a handful of times. Ava's had doctor's appointments, and then sometimes I just enjoy getting out for a walk. I've run into Cal a few times, but all we've talked about is how my case is proceeding. Warren's been served all the papers, and now it's just a waiting game.

Thanksgiving is coming up, and Donna says it's a big deal here at the house. All the women cook and eat together. She says it's a step forward celebrating a holiday about family. Most of us have come from a broken family/relationship. It helps to be around people who understand, but always ones who will help build new memories.

Donna told me she had a special guest coming to lunch. I have no idea who she means, but all I can think about is that Roni is supposed to come by tonight with news. She called this morning, and said she needed to talk to me, but wanted to do it in person.

I've been pacing the office for the last hour since I hung up the phone. I have no idea what could be so big that I need to see her in person, but it has me chewing my nails and wearing the carpet thin.

"You ok?" Donna rounded the corner. She's been working the early shift this week.

"Sure. I guess. Not really." I shrugged as I paced some more.

"Why don't you sit?" Donna pointed to my chair.

"I don't think that will make it better." I sighed. "Time needs to speed up, at least for this afternoon," I muttered.

"Don't wish time away. That little girl will grow up fast enough," Donna lamented.

"I know. I just need to know what Roni has to tell me." I flung my arms out in exasperation.

"Why don't you come help me with dinner. It'll make the time pass faster, and give you something to do." Donna smiled as she left the office.

oooooooooo

Dinner was consumed rather quickly tonight. We had burgers, a house favorite. Most of the women had gone to their rooms after eating, but I was watching out the front window. It was strange; I used to do this when I lived with Warren, and now I found myself doing it here.

Headlights shown through the curtains just as I was getting ready to give up. I assumed that Roni had something come up, and needed to reschedule. I watched out the window, and she climbed out of her car. She trotted up the steps, but before she could knock, I swung the door open.

"You're fast. I almost knocked on your face." Roni smiled.

"Come in." I moved out of the way. I was trying not to sound too eager, but I was dying to know what the news was.

"He signed away his rights." She thrust a folder in my direction. "Ava is yours, and he can't take her away."

"Are you serious?" I clasped my hand over my mouth as I sat down on the couch. "But the assistance? He contested it? He said she was his dependent?" I was so confused.

"I don't know. These were delivered today by courier. Signed and sealed. He doesn't want rights to her. You can get your assistance now, and he can't stop it." I was so overcome, I flung myself into her arms. "See why I didn't want to tell you this over the phone?" She laughed lightly.

"Yes!" I nodded vigorously. "What about the divorce?"

"That's going to take a little while. He's refusing to sign at the moment," she grumbled.

"What? Why?" my forehead crinkled in confusion.

"No idea. Some of these men are complete assholes. They fight until they either run out of time, or money. Fortunately, your time apart counts toward separation."

"Warren has plenty of money," I murmured. "What now?"

"I'm going to call his attorney in the morning and see why he's refusing. It could be that he just wants something you have." She shrugged.

"Like what? My clothes? I don't have anything!" I raised my voice in frustration.

"I get it, I do. I'll see why he's holding out and let you know. We may not get an answer though, so don't hold your breath," she warned.

"Ok." I punched the cushion beside me. Warren was doing this to be a douche. He didn't want to be married to me. This was his last form of control. He knew that as long as he didn't give in, I wouldn't get what I wanted.

"Try to look at the positive, Brooke. You've got full custody of your daughter. He gave her to you with no strings. He can't take her away, and if you find someone later on down the road, she'll be able to be adopted." Roni put her arm around my shoulder and hugged me.

"You're right." I nodded. "I need to stay positive. He's done enough. This won't last. If I don't give in, he'll get tired of it and let it go too."

"Yes. Think like that. These things take time, and I'm going to get it moving as fast as I can, but that still may be slower than you want." She started to stand as Donna walked in.

"Everything ok in here?" Donna leaned against the doorway.

"As good as they can be, I guess. He gave up his rights to Ava." I smiled.

"That's great. I mean, not really, great, but this way you don't have to fight that." She offered a sad smile. "No child should have to grow up with only one parent, but it can be done."

"I'm pretty sure she'd only have one parent even if he was involved. Warren's too selfish to be a dad," I grumbled. "He was a sperm donor at most."

Both Donna and Roni laughed. "You're right. I didn't want to be the one to say it, but you're right." Roni laughed harder.

"Are you doing anything for the holiday?" Donna smiled.

"Probably working. There's an opening for partner in the firm. There are three of us who want it." She sighed.

"You should come over if you can." I shifted on my feet. "Donna says it's going to be a real feast."

"I'm sure it will be. You haven't had one of Donna's famous Thanksgiving lunches." Roni grinned. "I've gotta head out, but I'll keep you posted on the dirtbag. Try and stay positive."

"I will. Thanks." I held my hand out for Roni to shake, but instead she wrapped me in a hug.

"You're doing it, Brooke. You're surviving. Pretty soon it'll be more than that... you'll be living." Roni whispered the words before releasing me.

I mashed my lips together to keep from crying. She was right. I was surviving. I was spending every day convincing myself that I could do this. I could raise my daughter on my own. I could live without Warren breathing down my neck. I could be me. I was stronger than I knew. I could endure the storm to dance in the rainbow.

Chapter 11

Brooke

"Brooke?" I could hear Amy whisper shouting down the hallway.

"What?" I stuck my head out the door just in time for her to barge in, pushing me back in the process. "Is something wrong?" My forehead wrinkled as I watched her. I'd been getting Ava dressed, and Amy was now plastered to my door as if she was trying to keep someone out.

"Wrong? I don't know. I mean, I do know, but it's not the wrong you think it is. Am I making sense?" Her head tipped to the side as her lips pursed in concentration. "It doesn't seem like I am."

"No, you're not." I laughed lightly. "Should I be worried?"

"I don't think so." She shook her head slightly as she left her spot by the door and came over to the bed. "You have a visitor." She grinned. "A male visitor."

My back straightened as I thought about the possibility of one of Warren's friends coming to deliver a message for him. It would be just like him to do that. I quickly finished snapping up Ava's onesie and tucked her close to my chest.

"I can watch her for you, if you want." Amy reached for Ava.

"Ok," I slowly released my daughter. Everyone has been great about helping out, but it's hard. I love her so much, and I want to be with her all the time.

Amy sat down on the bed and began talking to Ava as I slowly opened my door. I inched down the hallway like a small child would, trying to peer into the living room without being seen. I heard laughter as I grew closer, and my anxiety eased. "I don't know what's taking so long. Amy might have gotten sidetracked. Let me go look," Donna's voice sounded.

She rounded the corner and almost bumped into me. "Oh, there you are. You have a guest." She motioned to the living room and then scooted around me.

I hadn't heard anyone else so I was more confused than ever, but sped up hoping to solve this mystery. When I crossed the threshold, there he was sitting on the couch. He stood and held out his hand. "I'm sorry for not calling you first, but I realized today that I don't have a number for you."

"Oh." I shook his hand. "Did you need something, Blake?" When I pulled my hand back, I wrapped my arms around my middle. I suddenly felt exposed and was really lost on why he'd be here.

"No." He ran his hands through his hair as if he was frustrated or something. I knew the signs. I'd seen them with Warren. "I'm messing this up. I'm sorry." He tugged at the sides before standing up and stepping closer. "My shift ended, and I wasn't ready to go home yet. I thought you might like to join me for a cup of coffee."

I could feel the shock that must have been all over my face. "Coffee? Um, we have coffee here, and I have Ava to take care of. I just... I don't know," I stammered.

"That's ok." His head dropped in defeat. "It was just an idea. Maybe another time." He turned to leave, but Donna came scurrying into the room.

"I'll watch Ava for you. You should go," she urged and gave me a look that said I better listen.

"Are you sure?" My voice shook.

"'Course I'm sure." She pointed to my coat. "Bundle up. It's cold out."

I glanced between Blake and Donna. "If you're sure it's ok."

"It's fine," Donna insisted. She moved closer and whispered in my ear. "It's just coffee. It's a good place to start. Trust your instincts. Think about what we've discussed in group."

"Right." I nodded. She was right. It was JUST coffee. I reached for my coat on the hook by the door, but Blake was faster. He held it out for me to slip into, and then opened the door and held it for me. I stood there stiff for a moment as it all sank in. I'd never had someone so chivalrous before. Warren usually just plowed ahead and left me to fend for myself.

It took a minute to move, and Blake looked perplexed as he watched me. "I won't keep her out late." He smiled at Donna, and then closed the door behind us. We walked down the steps and turned right on the sidewalk. The sun was setting, and the sky was a beautiful shade of purple. Winter was coming fast, and the air had a bite to it. I pulled my coat tighter as I shivered against the breeze.

"I'm sorry for just showing up like that." Blake smiled softly as he glanced over at me. "I know I probably caught you by surprise, but I thought you might need a friend." He shrugged.

"A friend?" I glanced up at him and then back at my feet.

"Yeah. I mean, I know you have all the girls, but some things you need a guy's perspective on, ya know?" He laughed lightly. "I know you're not ready for more, Brooke." His voice trailed off as we approached a crosswalk. It was as if he could read my mind. I wasn't ready. I wasn't sure I ever would be.

"Thanks." I offered a sad smile. "For understanding. I think something might be wrong with me."

"Wrong? Like what?" He reached for my hand as the light turned green and we stepped out on to the street to cross.

"I didn't see the signs. I thought he was a good guy. I was so wrong." I sighed.

"Guys like him are good at hiding it. At first, they don't think there's anything wrong with them, and when they figure out there is, they learn to hide it. I promise you that there is nothing wrong with you. He taught you to hide it too. He used that fear you had to force you into submission."

"Donna told us in group that we have to learn to take chances. I just don't know if I'll ever be ready for that. I know that I'm not ready now," I lamented. We'd reached the coffee shop at this point, and Blake held the door open as we stepped into the warmth. This was the same place where I'd run into Cal when I'd seen Warren outside. That was the last time I'd seen him, but I'd be a fool to think that it wouldn't happen again.

As we made our way to the counter, Blake stepped behind me. "I understand, Brooke. I do. I don't want to push you into anything you're not ready for. I just want to be your friend."

My shoulders relaxed as a calm feeling began to settle over me. It was something about Blake that did this. He didn't have to do or say anything. When we were near each other, I just felt safe. It was an odd feeling for me, and something I couldn't explain. As the line moved up, we stood there not speaking. By the time we reached the counter, I knew what I wanted.

"Caramel swirl with cream." I glanced back at Blake.

"House blend, black." He smiled.

"Eight seventy-five." The barista pulled two cups out and marked our order on the side. Blake paid, and then we moved to the end of the counter to wait.

"How do you drink black coffee?" I made a yuck face.

"I could ask you the same thing about the sweet stuff." His face twisted and I couldn't help but laugh. It was simple, but that's what I needed it to be. I needed the small things to work before the big ones ever could. Things like coffee and conversation were a big step for me. I wanted to believe that this could go somewhere, but I wasn't ready for that. The fact that Blake understood this made it so much easier.

"Wanna grab a seat over there?" He motioned to some small tables in the back corner.

"Sure." I turned and let him lead us. When we reached the table closest to the corner, Blake pulled out a chair for me. "Thank you." I set my coffee on the table and waited for him to sit across from me.

He scanned the coffee shop before sitting, and shrugged out of his coat. Other than when he helped me move, I'd never seen Blake not in doctor gear. Now, it was different. He sat there in a burgundy sweater with a light blue shirt peeking out of the collar. The sleeves were rolled slightly, and he was wearing navy pants. His sandy hair was tousled from his hands running through it. If I wasn't so messed up, I might have a hard time staying away from him. His blue eyes sparkled when he smiled; as he sat there just watching me, I could tell that this friendship was going to be an important one.

ooooooooo

Blake

I couldn't help but stare at her. She was beautiful. It's that kind of beauty that's natural. Brooke could wear a paper bag dress with no makeup and her hair a mess and she'd still be beautiful. I'd seen her at her worst. Now she was slowly becoming the woman who she was always meant to be, and every time I saw her, I wished for just five minutes in a room with her husband.

"How's Ava been doing since you brought her home?" I knew talking about Ava was a safe topic. It was something that she didn't clam up about.

She smiled and glanced up from where she'd been staring at her cup. "She's been doing great. She's sleeping more, and eating like crazy. It's hard for me to leave her to do anything. I don't know what I'm going to do when I have to send her to daycare."

"That's great. Don't rush things. Enjoy your time now. You've got plenty of it. Donna loves having you as an office manager. She talks about it all the time at the hospital." I laughed lightly as I remembered Donna going on and on the other day about what a lifesaver Brooke has been. She told a story about how she couldn't find a bill that needed to be paid, only to find out that Brooke had already mailed it.

"I like it there. It's the first place I've felt safe, and had real friends." She nodded as she sipped her coffee. We sat there in quiet conversation until we'd both finished our drinks.

It was getting dark out, and the wind was starting to pick up. "You ready to head back? It's looking like it might snow."

"Snow? Already?" Isn't it kinda early?" She watched out the window like a small child would.

"It's a little early, but I remember getting snow early in years past." I stood and reached for her empty cup to toss it out.

"The days all ran together in that house. I tried to not think about what day it was. It just made time go slower," she muttered as she stood and slipped her coat back on.

"I'm sorry." I cringed. I didn't know what else to say.

"It's ok." She followed me as we weaved through the tables and back to the door. I pushed it open, and she stepped outside and turned slightly to wait for me. After tossing the cups into the can by the door, I joined her on the sidewalk. "Thanks for this." She smiled softly.

"It was nothing." I lifted my arms slightly.

"It was everything to me. This is the first time a man has been nice to me that I won't be punished for. Warren was a jealous man. If anyone was nice to me, especially a man, he accused me of cheating. I've never been able to experience what we just did." She wrapped her arms around her middle and shivered.

"Come here." I motioned her closer. "Is this ok?" I gently placed my arm around her back and pulled her closer. She went stiff but I waited. "Tell me if this isn't ok." I looked her right in the eyes and waited.

"You're warm," she murmured as her body slowly relaxed against my side.

"That was the idea. You've been shivering since we stepped outside." I started to move us down the sidewalk.

"Thanks, Blake." She leaned her head against my shoulder and sighed. I didn't say anything, just continued to walk although every part of me wanted to say something. I wanted to give her this. Her perfect evening; something she said she'd never had.

We walked in silence back to the house, and when we got to the steps, I stopped. This wasn't a date, at least for her it wasn't. Going inside wouldn't do anything but make it awkward. "Thanks for coming tonight. I enjoyed it." I released her and waited.

"Me too." She smiled.

"Maybe next time we can get something to eat." I stepped back, giving her space.

"I'd like that." She moved up the steps.

"Goodnight, Brooke." I waited.

"Night, Blake." She opened the door and disappeared inside. I stood there just staring at the house for several minutes. I wondered what she was doing. Was she talking to the other girls? Was she spending time with Ava? Was she thinking about me, and the friendship I'd proposed? I wasn't paying attention to my surroundings as I turned to walk back to the hospital or I would have been more prepared.

"Stay away from my wife." It was a deep, menacing voice. I turned just in time to come face to face with a fist heading straight for my right cheek. I stumbled back and blinked several times as I stared at him. He wasn't a big guy. We'd met the first time he'd brought Brooke into the ER.

"She's mine, I know it and she knows it. You keep your fucking hands off her!" He turned and stormed away as I pulled my phone from my pocket to dial my brother. Warren wasn't supposed to be within a hundred feet of Brooke, and the front lawn of the house was definitely within a hundred feet.

Chapter 12

Blake

As I made my way back to the hospital, snow flurries began to fall. My face was throbbing, and I could feel my eye swelling shut. 'Great. I'm on call tonight for the ER. How can one perform surgery if one can't see?' When I reached the ambulance bay, I pulled my cell from my coat pocket.

"S'up?" Cal 's voice sounded from the other end of the line.

"I need to file a report." I sighed. "I was assaulted tonight."

"What?" Cal suddenly got serious. "When? How?"

"I'm fine. Thanks for asking," I muttered as I shifted. "I took Brooke for coffee. Her husband saw us, and took a swing at me. I wanna press charges."

"Ok. Where are you? Can you come to the station?" I could hear him fumbling around with something.

"I'm at work. My shift starts in just a few minutes. Can I come by after my shift?" I glanced at my watch. I had less than five minutes before I was supposed to make rounds, and then I had to be in the ER.

"Sure. Pressing charges will help her case." A loud crash sounded and Cal muttered something. "Did she witness this?"

"No. She was inside. He came up to me outside the house." I started walking inside.

"So he broke the order of protection?" Cal's voice climbed.

"Yes." I nodded. I knew he couldn't see me.

"I've got to let her lawyer know. I need to pick him up. Breaking that means he goes to lock up." More noise and I could tell Cal was moving.

"I gotta go, Bro. My shift started, and I'm still in the ambulance bay."

"Ok. Call me when you're on your way. I'll get everything filled out, and you can sign your statement." The line went dead, and I slipped my phone back into my pocket.

ooooooooo

I rushed through the ER toward the elevators. I wanted to get up to my office to grab the files I needed for rounds. Just as I stepped onto one, one of the residents followed me.

"Evening, Dr. Blake." She smiled up at me. Jenny's always been a flirt, and tonight was no different.

"Hi." I glanced at my watch and tapped my foot. I hated being late.

"Yikes! What happened to your face?" She cringed.

"Does it look that bad?" I touched it lightly. I was starting to get a headache, and it was really tender. "You should see the other guy."

"No crazy story like walking into a door while reading?" She giggled. One of our other neurologists was notorious for reading files while walking. He's fallen down the stairs from it.

"No, nothing like that." I sighed. Right at that moment, the doors opened on my floor and I rushed off. I scurried down the hall toward my office, ignoring the strange looks I was getting from the staff. I didn't want to explain myself, and I didn't have the time anyway.

Once inside, I closed the door, and rushed into my private bathroom. I clipped my pager on my belt in case I got called, and then flicked the lights on. Upon seeing my reflection, I knew why Jenny reacted the way she did. My eye was swollen, and my cheek was an angry red. I was sure to have a bruise. I used my fingers to feel along my eye socket. Nothing felt broken, it just hurt. I cursed myself for not reacting quickly enough. After slipping into my lab coat, I rushed to the closest nurse's station. Luckily, it was empty. I grabbed a cold pack, activated it, and held it to my face as I rushed back to the ER.

My night was uneventful, and as the sun began to rise, I yawned and made my way back upstairs. I needed to make a quick change, and then head to my brother's district. He said it wouldn't take long, and I hoped he was right. I haven't slept in thirty-six hours, and I'm starting to feel it.

ooooooooo

Brooke

I haven't left the house today. When I woke up, I lifted my blinds to see Warren standing across the street. He's exactly a hundred feet away. He can't legally come any closer, but he won't leave either. I don't know when he showed up. Donna told me to ignore it. She said as long as he doesn't try to come closer, I shouldn't be in any danger.

Roni called this morning. She said she was going to stop over on her lunch break. Since Warren was staking the place out, she thought it better for her to come to me. She said she had some leverage for my case, but I have no idea what that is.

"He still out there?" Amy leaned against my door.

"Yeah." I sighed as I tickled Ava's belly. She's been staying awake more now, and actually playing with me.

"Wanna hang out downstairs with me? I don't have to be at work for another hour." Amy motioned to the hallway.

"Sure. That beats being stuck in here." I lifted Ava into my arms, grabbed her baby seat, and headed to the family room. Just as I was settling Ava into her seat, Lauren, another woman at the house, came rushing in.

"There's something going on outside." She pointed to the front window. "Did one of you call the cops?"

Amy and I both looked at each other, "no." We scrambled to get over to the window and what I saw brought relief and a little satisfaction. Warren was being handcuffed and placed in the back of a cruiser.

"I thought he had a hundred feet?" Amy looked at me, perplexed.

"He does. Maybe this is something else," I mused.

"You think he's done something to someone else?" Amy glanced at me, and then turned to stare back out the window. Ava cooed as her baby seat bounced from the floor. I stared, unblinking, as I watched Warren get man handled as he was forced into the backseat of a cruiser. His gaze never wavered from staring at the house, and at one point I thought we made eye contact. I shivered as memories of that stare rushed through me. It was the same look he gave as a warning whenever people were around. It meant 'just you wait until we're alone. I'm coming for you.'

"Isn't that the guy who helped you move?" Lauren pointed to one of the officers. I couldn't see his face at the moment, but he did seem familiar.

After the back door to the cruiser was closed, the officer turned around. It was Cal. He waved at the house, and smiled softly. It was as if he was telling me that everything was going to be ok. As the cruiser pulled away, Cal jogged across the street, and up the walk to the house.

Before he got to the door, I flung it open. "What happened?" I looked past him at the group of cops all slowly leaving the scene.

"He assaulted someone last night. They pressed charges, and we had reports that he broke the order of protection. He's heading to central booking now." Cal touched my shoulder. "You're safe. He's not getting out for a few days at least, maybe longer."

"You wanna come in?" I stepped back, but Cal shook his head.

"Gotta head back and process the paperwork for him. I just wanted to come over and tell you that he won't be bothering you for a few days, minimum."

"Thanks." I waved as Cal made his way back to his car across the street.

"Looks like you can go outside after all." Amy smiled.

"Yeah. I just wonder who he assaulted. I'm the only person he's ever hit in the past. Did he find someone new already?" I lowered myself onto the couch and stared off into the distance.

"I don't think that's the case at all. I'm sure we can find out though." Amy placed her arm around me. "Don't be sad.

Whatever happened wasn't your fault and it'll help your case."

"I know. I know I shouldn't feel bad, but I can't help it. He hurt someone like he used to hurt me. It scares me to know he's started going after others. At least when I was there it was just me."

"Stop." Donna came into the room. "You stop thinking like that right now. This isn't your fault. Think about what we've talked about in group. You've come a long way since leaving him; don't go backwards. You're doing what you can to heal you. You can't think about anyone else right now. You and Ava are your priority."

"You're right." I slowly nodded.

"Of course, I am." Donna grinned.

"Thanks, guys. I think I'm gonna go lie down for a bit before Roni gets here." I lifted Ava, and headed back to my room. I needed to process all of this in a quiet place.

ooooooooo

"Knock knock." Roni stuck her head through the door of my room. "I hope this is ok. Donna told me to come on back."

"Sure." I yawned. When Ava had fallen asleep, I'd napped too. I hadn't realized how tired I was just from stress.

"We can talk in here." Roni pulled the chair I had in the corner closer, and sat down. "First, I wanted to let you know that Warren was arrested this morning."

"I saw that from the front window," I mumbled.

"Well, I'm planning to use jail time as a bargaining chip for signing the divorce papers. I've talked to the DA and they're willing to play ball along with the other victim. Since this is a first offense, the judge will probably grant probation and some type of community service. If the other victim wants to go to court, we can get assault three which comes with jail time of up to two years. I figured Warren won't want to go to jail, so he'll sign."

"So, that's it? He gets off if he signs?" I was confused. Did I want that?

"Not really. He'll still be punished; it just won't be as severe." Roni smiled. "This is good, Brooke. Believe me, this is what we need."

"Ok. If you believe that this is the best option, then I'm ok with it. I just want to move on. I want to live my life and not worry about him." I glanced towards the window where the afternoon sun was starting to peek through.

"I'll draft up a proposal and get this right over to his lawyer. We should get a response in a few days." She stood, tucked the papers back in her briefcase, and walked out the door.

Was this really as good as Roni said it was? Would I be able to accept Warren being free, when he could serve time? Was the other victim really ok with this? I mean, they got hurt. I knew what that felt like, and I knew what it was like to not get any reparations for it. Why did it always seem that no matter what, Warren was lurking in the background? How much more was I going to have to endure?

Chapter 13

Brooke

I've spent the last couple of days in a fog. Roni sent our proposal to Warren's lawyer, and now we wait. The waiting is the worst part. There's no timeline, and Warren knows that the longer he takes, the worse it is for me. He used to keep me on pins and needles all the time when we were first married. He'd tell me that we 'might' be doing something or someone 'might' be coming over. I was expected to be ready regardless if it happened or not. The first time I thought he was joking around. The black eye I received said he wasn't. Now, even though we're living apart, he's still pulling this crap.

"Brooke. Blake is here." Amy stuck her head in the office. It was the middle of the day, and I wasn't expecting him. I frowned as I stood up and made my way to the family room. When I rounded the corner, I was shocked at what I saw. Blake had a giant bruise on his cheek. It was a greenish purple color like it was a few days old.

"Hey." He waved when he saw me, but I just stood there staring. "You should see the other guy." He chuckled, but I still couldn't move. "Brooke." He held out his arms as he approached. "I'm fine. Really."

"These hurt." I lifted my hand and gently touched his cheek. He stood there not moving a muscle, letting me touch his face. When I pulled my hand back, he released a shuddered sigh as though he was in pain.

"I'm fine," he whispered and his mouth curled up on one side. "I was thinking you might like to grab a coffee before I go on shift."

"Sure. Let me get my coat." I smiled softly as I turned and walked back to my room. Ava was fast asleep in her crib. I grabbed the monitor and my coat, and headed back to the family room. Lauren was reading on the couch. "Can you keep an ear out for her? She just went down, and should sleep until I get back."

"No problem." Lauren set the monitor on the table beside her.

"Thanks." I slipped my coat on and turned toward Blake. "We can't be out long. I need to be here when she wakes."

"We'll be quick. I just want to talk to you about something," Blake promised as he opened the door and let me pass.

ooooooooo

It didn't take long to get to the coffee shop, and when we did it was surprisingly empty. "So, is this going to be our thing?" I glanced up at him as we stood in line. I couldn't help but stare at the bruise.

"It can be." He smiled. "I'm always up for coffee with a beautiful woman." I blushed and turned away. I couldn't help it. I wasn't used to being complimented. "It's the truth." He nudged my shoulder as we moved up in line.

91

After ordering our coffees, we made our way to a table in the back. Soft music filled the air along with the clicking of laptop keys. This was a popular place for young professionals to work while they snacked. "I'm surprised it isn't more crowded."

"This is an odd time. Usually the rush is around meal time. We're in between that," Blake mused as he sat across from me. "I guess I should tell you about this before you stare a hole in my face." He laughed lightly.

"I'm sorry," I murmured. "I just know how bad those hurt." I cringed as Blake seemed startled by my response.

"Your ex hit me. He saw us the last time we came here. This was a warning, apparently." He shrugged.

"A warning for what?" I gasped.

"To stay away." Blake rolled his eyes. "I'm not staying away, Brooke. We're friends, and your asshole husband doesn't get a say in who you are friends with."

"You're the victim Roni was talking about." The words tumbled from my mouth as my head tried to make sense of it all. The pieces were clicking together and light bulbs were flashing. Blake was the reason that my divorce would go through. He was the one pressing charges.

"Yes." He sipped his coffee and nodded.

"You're the one who agreed to less jail time so she could pressure him to sign." I stared at my cup in front of me.

"Yes." He nodded again. "Before you start worrying or over thinking this any more than you already are… I'm not losing here. I'm ok with this. It was my choice. A bruised cheek isn't keeping me from anything, but those papers are. I really like hanging out with you, Brooke, and I want you to want to hang out with me more. I know that won't happen as long as he's still part of your life. If letting him get off easy helps you, then I'll do it."

"You need to think about what you're giving up. You could send him to jail." I gasped.

"There's no thinking about it. I'm doing this so you can have your freedom. I want you and Ava to have a fresh start. I'd like to be a part of it too, but I'm ok if I'm not." He smiled as he reached across the table and squeezed my hand.

"I didn't know men like you still existed." I sniffed. My emotions were overwhelming me and I needed air. "Can we start walking back? Ava will be up soon."

"Sure." He stood, slipped into his coat, and then helped me with mine. "Are we ok?" He glanced at me as he held the door open for us. I still wasn't used to his chivalrous ways.

"What do you mean?" I furrowed my brow.

"I mean, are things ok with us? Are you gonna push me away, or are we still friends?" He was gesturing with his hands as we walked and seemed to be getting slightly frustrated. I couldn't understand why either.

"I guess." I tipped my head to the side and looked up at him. His brow creased as his lips thinned. He sighed heavily and then kinda shook his head.

"You're doing it again," I muttered as I too shook my head in frustration.

"Doing what?" He came to a halt and stepped closer to the building we were currently walking by.

"Acting weird. You did it when I moved out, and then again at the coffee shop when I ran into Cal. What am I doing that's upsetting you?" I crossed my arms and shivered against the cold.

"You're cold. Let's just get back." He motioned toward the house. We were still two blocks away.

"No." I stared up at him. "Warren did this all the time. He'd get mad at me, and then he wouldn't tell me why. I can't fix the problem if I don't know what the problem is." I rolled my eyes. "So, what am I doing wrong?"

We stood there staring at each other, neither giving in. Finally, he broke. "You're not doing anything wrong. I'm the one who's wrong," he growled.

"You?" I was confused.

"Yeah. I don't like thinking about you with someone else. You and my brother. You and that asshole of an ex. You with anyone." His eyes flared.

"But I'm not with anyone." I shivered again.

"I know that, but I think you should be. You should be with someone who treats you like a queen. You need a man to cook for you; to rub your feet after a long day; to help with Ava; to tell you how beautiful you are when you first wake up and then again before you fall asleep. You need a man who will love you the way a man is supposed to love a woman. You deserve it, and I just want you to know that." He stepped around me, putting himself between me and the street. Without even asking, he reached down and took my hand in his. He started walking, and I followed without question. I don't know why, but I always feel safe with Blake.

"What does all that mean?" I panted slightly. I was out of breath from the pace he was keeping. "What you said back there. What does that mean?"

We reached the front lawn of the house and stopped. I yanked lightly on his hand until he looked at me. I lifted my chin, silently telling him to answer me. His lips pressed together fighting to hold back the words, but I don't think he could have no matter how hard he tried. "It means, I know you need friends right now. I know that you're not ready, but when you are… I'm here. I want to be that man, Brooke. I wanna cook for you. I wanna snuggle on the couch in front of a fire with snow outside. I want to help with Ava. I've been holding it in for weeks because I'm afraid of what telling you all this is going to do to us, but I'm ready to take a chance. If I can ask you to take a leap of faith with me, then I should be able to do the same." He stepped back and smiled a boyish smile. "I want you to think about all of this. Take as long as you need, and when you're ready for it, I'll be there. In the meantime, we're gonna keep getting coffee and talking."

Just as I was about to say something, the door opened. "Ava just woke up," Lauren blurted out and then slapped her hand over her mouth when she realized she'd interrupted. "Sorry," she murmured.

"It's ok." Blake smiled as he started to walk backwards. "I have to get to work anyway. Think about what I said." He waved and then turned and left.

I stood there for a few moments, just watching his back as he grew smaller and smaller. I'd never met a man like him. Every time we've met up, he's given me a little piece of myself back. He's taught me that I am worthy of attention and affection. I just needed to decide if I was ready.

Chapter 14

Brooke

Blake has kept his word. He's come by a few times over the last week for coffee outings. I can't call them dates because we're just friends, but I honestly don't know how a date with him would be different. He holds doors for me, pulls out my chair, and always pays. I've thought about what he said on the front lawn several thousand times over these last few days, but today I've been too busy.

Today is Thanksgiving, and Donna has had us all up preparing for our feast since a little after sunrise. I woke to her humming in the kitchen as she prepped the turkey. Amy has been cleaning and straightening the house, and Lauren already had stuffing made, and was starting on the cranberries last I checked.

"Can you help me get this box down?" Amy motioned to a large box on the top shelf in the hall closet. "I think the good napkins and tablecloth are in there."

"Sure." I smiled as I met her at the door. Amy was petite, and this was a tall shelf. I could barely reach it when I stood on my tiptoes. "You'd think we were expecting the queen." I laughed as the box slowly slid into my hands. "All this for just us." I shrugged. Three of the other girls at the house had to work, so there was just going to be the four of us for lunch. Becky, Carol, and Megan would have to reheat plates when they got home.

"Donna didn't tell you?" Amy smirked. "We have guests coming today. She invited some friends from the hospital." Amy's voice said she wasn't telling me the entire truth. She grinned as she took the box from me and scurried down the hallway.

"Wait, what?" I skipped off after her. "Who from the hospital?" Just as Amy set the box on the table, Ava let out a yelp. She'd been napping for a while, so I knew it was bound to happen.

"Saved by the baby." Amy giggled as I sighed and turned to head toward my room.

"I'll be back," I warned before slipping away to check on my daughter.

ooooooooo

The morning went by rather quickly. It was a beautiful fall day. Cold, but sunny with a bright blue sky. It was a welcome sight after all the gray gloomy days we'd had earlier in the week.

I was sitting on the couch talking to Ava when there was a knock at the door. "I'll be right back." I smiled at her as I placed her in her bouncy chair on the floor. I clicked a few buttons to turn on the music, and then got up to answer the door. "Who is it?" I called.

"It's Veronica." Roni's voice sounded from the other side. I opened the door happily. I hadn't seen or heard from Roni in over a week. "Happy Thanksgiving." She smiled.

"Same to you. Are you here to eat with us?" I glanced around. I wasn't sure who would be coming by after what Amy said.

"No. I still have a few briefs to get together before the next week. I usually go to my parents' place late and eat leftovers." She smiled as she thrust a manila envelope in my direction. "I thought I'd give you a little holiday treat early." She grinned even wider. "Open it."

My fingers fumbled with the clasp as I slowly backed up and glanced at Ava. I pulled the papers from the envelope and read the words typed at the top of the first page. "The dissolution of marriage between Brooke Ellis and Warren Ellis. Is this real?" I gasped.

"No, silly. I'm giving you fake divorce papers." Roni rolled her eyes before she started laughing. "Of course, they're real."

"He signed? I'm free?" I stumbled farther into the house. It was as if a giant weight had been taken off my shoulders. My heart felt lighter as tears leaked from my eyes. Roni grabbed my elbow as I started to crumple to the floor. She carefully walked me over to the couch, and closed the door.

"It's over." She smiled. "You're free." She held my hands in hers. We both laughed as I cried. It was a feeling that I wasn't expecting, freedom. It had been so long since I'd had it, I wasn't sure I'd know what to do. "The order of protection is still good. It doesn't expire until the end of the year. If you don't feel safe by then, then we can file to renew it."

"I don't know how to thank you." I cried.

"You don't need to thank me. I'm happy I could help you. Just promise me you'll be happy. That's all I ask of you." She started to stand.

"I will." I nodded as I clutched the papers in my hands. "I'll be happy and I'll always remember this." I glanced at Ava and then back at Roni. "Thank you. Thank you from me and from her. She doesn't know it yet, but you're her hero." I sobbed. Roni nodded as she pressed her lips together. I could tell she was getting emotional too. "Emily would be proud," I added just as she reached the door. She nodded again, before disappearing out the door.

ooooooooo

Blake

Do you think this is ok?" I held up a sweater in front of my webcam. I was trying to get advice from my brother, but he was sucking at it.

"Sure." He shrugged. "The last five you showed me looked fine too."

"You're no help," I grumbled as I tossed yet another sweater onto my bed.

"You're acting like a girl. Who cares what you wear? She'd probably like it better if you didn't wear clothes."

"I'm not there yet." I sighed. I'd been thinking about it every time I talked to her. I see her hips sway as she walks down the steps at the house and my dick twitches. It was dying to know what she looked like under all the clothes.

"And why not?" Cal smirked.

"Because she's still married. I'm not into going after married women. I don't care how crappy their husbands are. I'm not going to do it," I growled as I pulled out a blue shirt. "What about this?"

"Sure." Cal shrugged again.

"You said that about the last one," I huffed.

"Dude. You wanna know what I'm wearing?" He chuckled and then stood up. "This." He pointed at the t-shirt he was wearing. It had a Captain America symbol on it. "I got jeans on the bottom half."

"It's Thanksgiving." My forehead crinkled. "You can't pick something nicer?"

"Ok, Mom." His head tipped to the side as he stared at me through the screen. "I wear dress pants and a button down to work almost every day. I like to be comfortable when I'm off duty." He lifted his hands in the air as if to say 'can you blame me'.

"Fine," I grumbled. "I'll see you at two."

"Later." He gave a finger wave as he laughed before the connection broke and my screen went black. Maybe Cal had a point. Maybe I was trying too hard. Maybe I should just go casual.

I rummaged through my closet until I found my Eastside University Crew team shirt. It was a favorite, and that was obvious by the amount of wear it had seen. The yellow lettering on the maroon fabric was faded and the cotton was super soft from all the washes it had endured. I grabbed a pair of jeans, combed my hair, and slapped a little cologne on. I didn't want to look like a total slob, but I did want to be comfortable. Brooke saw me in dress clothes every time we hung out. Maybe if I looked a little more approachable, I might get her to relax a little around me.

ooooooooo

"Glad to see you were finally able to make a choice," Cal shouted as he jogged down the steps of his apartment building. He had a hoodie on with the hood pulled up.

"If we weren't on our way right now, I'd give you something to laugh about," I grumbled as I stuffed my hands into my pockets. It was cold out today.

"I'm parked over here." Cal motioned as he started walking around the corner. We entered the lot for residents of his building and slipped into his Mustang. "You know, maybe if you bought a car like this, she'd notice you a little more."

"I like my Audi just fine, and why would I want a woman who only likes me for my clothes and car?" I shook my head as Cal took a corner a little too fast and my shoulder bumped the door. "Slow down." I gave him a side eye.

"Stop being such a girl today." Cal rolled his eyes.

"It's called being responsible. You know… that thing I have to do all the time. Being the big brother isn't as easy as you think. I was always covering for you growing up," I muttered just as Cal parked in front of Emily's House.

"I wasn't that bad." He chuckled as he flung his door open and climbed out.

"Sure. Sure, you weren't!" I yelled at his back, but he was already up the stairs and knocking on the door.

oooooooooo

Brooke

We'd just finished setting the food out when there was a knock at the door. "I'll get it," Lauren called as she left the dining room. In a matter of seconds, she was back with Cal and Blake. "Our dinner guests have arrived."

"Glad you guys could make it." Donna smiled. "Take a seat." Cal grabbed a seat on the end, but Blake continued to stand awkwardly in the doorway.

"Aren't you going to eat?" I set the baby monitor by a plate and slowly sat. Ava had fallen asleep just a little bit ago, and I wanted to be able to get up easily if I needed to.

"Of course. I was waiting for everyone else to sit." He smiled as he took the seat right beside me. There were six of us, and we were sitting around a table made for four, so it was a tight fit. Blake was wearing jeans, and when he sat beside me his thigh was pressed right up against mine. I could feel the rough denim through the cotton of my leggings and it put my body on high alert.

Blake made me feel like a schoolgirl, and the last few times I've seen him, I wondered if he still meant everything he'd told me that day walking home from the coffee shop.

"Is this ok?" he murmured into my ear.

"Is what ok?" I whispered back.

"Me being here." He reached for a dish of beans the same time I did, and our hands brushed.

"Yes." It came out sounding breathless. My heart was racing, and it felt like every hair on my body was standing on end.

"You don't seem ok." He drew his hand back and turned slightly, causing our knees to bump.

I swallowed and closed my eyes. "I'm fine. Just been a busy day."

"I can see that." Blake motioned to the table full of food.

"No, not that. I got my divorce papers today. It's a lot to take in, that's all. Not you." I nodded as I scooped beans onto my plate.

"I see." His right hand slowly lifted and moved toward me. His eyes flared slightly as he settled his hand on my thigh painstakingly slow. I could feel how tense he was as a ragged breath escaped him. "Still ok?"

"Yes." I relaxed slightly and so did he. This was Blake, and even though we seemed to be moving into unchartered waters, I felt like I could do it with him. There was something about him that made me feel safe and wanted. He didn't know it then, but he was giving me something I'd never had…trust in a man.

Chapter 15

Brooke

Dinner seemed to go by in a blur. I don't really remember much about what was going on around me except for the fact that Blake's palm stayed right where he'd put it. Conversation buzzed about the room, but I wasn't listening. All my senses were tuned into Blake and what he was doing.

Just as Donna brought out the pumpkin pie, Ava woke up. She wasn't really crying, but more like whimpering and fussing. "Excuse me." I slowly stood, causing Blake to shift in his chair. "I'll be right back." I scurried out of the room, and rushed down the hall to my room.

Ava was waving her hands and feet in the air, and demanding food. "Hey, sweetie." I peered over the edge of her crib. "Let's get you changed, and then I'll feed you." I lifted her in the air, and smiled as she continued to kick her feet. Her sleeper made me laugh. It read 'Baby's first Thanksgiving' and had little pumpkins and turkeys all over it.

I laid her on my bed, and changed her diaper before making my way to the kitchen to mix a bottle. As I stood at the counter pouring water into a bottle, one handed I might add, I could hear the dinner conversation still going. Cal was cracking a joke, and everyone was laughing. I scooped some formula into the bottle, twisted the lid on, and shook it to mix. "One second." I glanced at Ava as I shifted her in my arms. She spotted the bottle, and her little arms flailed to get it. Her mouth opened, and as soon as I touched the nipple to her lips, she gave a hearty suck. Her eyes stared at me for a moment before she closed them to enjoy the bliss of being fed.

I shifted her in my arms one more time as I left the kitchen and headed back to the dining room. When I approached the table, Blake stood and pulled out my chair. I sat, and then he sat back down.

"I served you a piece of pie." He grimaced as he noticed that my hands were quite full at the moment.

"Thanks." I sighed.

"Can I feed her?" He motioned to where Ava was happily sucking away on the bottle.

"Sure." I shrugged. "She's going to scream when I take this away." I motioned to the now half empty bottle.

"That's ok. I can handle it." He laughed lightly as he leaned closer. I held her out toward him and as the nipple slipped from her lips, her eyes flew open and she let out a hearty scream. "Shhhh." Blake jiggled her lightly in his arms as he adjusted his grip. Ava blinked at him a few times as she settled down. I watched as Blake leaned back in his chair, and placed the bottle back in her mouth. He seemed so natural for not having any kids of his own. "Eat." He nodded toward the untouched pie still sitting in front of me.

"Thanks." I slid it closer and lifted a bite to my lips. It tasted heavenly, and it was the first time anyone other than me had fed Ava since she'd been home. Don't get me wrong, the other women here would help if I let them, but I want to do as much as I can for my daughter. She had such a rough start to the world.

I finished my pie about the same time that Ava finished her bottle. Blake waved me off as he set the empty bottle on the table, and lifted Ava to his shoulder. She settled in, nuzzling his neck as he patted her back. After releasing a healthy burp, she yawned and her eyes fluttered closed.

Blake stood, and carried her into the living room. I followed, not really sure of what to make of all this. He sat in the rocker, and began humming as he rocked my daughter. I was stunned, so stunned that I didn't realize that I was crying. Donna handed me a tissue and hugged my shoulder as she whispered, "They're not all bad," in my ear. I pressed my lips together and sat down on the couch.

"You're a natural with her," I mused.

"My professor in med school told me I missed my calling. She swore I should have been a pediatrician. I wanted to go the neuro route though." He laughed.

"She was right. You were great with her." I stared off in the direction of the hallway. I wasn't sure where to go from here. It seemed like we were at a crossroads and I was driving. I didn't know if I needed to turn, brake, or go straight ahead.

"There's no rush here." Blake swallowed. I guess he could see the struggle on my face. "We can go as slow as you need. Do you understand me, Brooke?" He lifted my chin with his finger.

I blinked a few times to clear the tears. "Yes." It came out like a whisper.

"I want this to work, and it will, just trust me." He leaned forward and brushed his lips across my forehead. They were soft, and my whole body shuddered at their contact. "I'm gonna go, but I'll be back tomorrow." He pulled back and smiled as he tucked a loose hair behind my ear. "I'm glad you got your papers. Happy Thanksgiving." He waved, and then stepped through the front door, just leaving me there in a daze.

Blake was like no other person that I'd ever met, and we'd only scratched the surface.

ooooooooo

After Blake left, we each helped Donna clean up the dining room. It was getting dark out, and everyone was sleepy from eating so much. Ava stayed quiet, so I used the time to sit in the family room and read. The house seemed cozier that night, and I wondered if it had anything to do with my mood. It was the first time in a long time that I wasn't scared. The freedom of knowing I was no longer tied to Warren opened a part of me I'd forgotten was there. Possibility and hope bloomed inside me, and for the first time since moving in here, I was excited for the next day. Blake said he'd be back, but I wasn't sure what that meant.

I'm not sure when it happened, but I fell asleep in the chair in the corner. I was awoken by Ava demanding her midnight bottle. Someone had covered me with a blanket and when I stood, I almost tripped.

I shuffled into the kitchen, half asleep, to mix a bottle. Then I headed to my room. Ava's cries were getting louder, causing me to move faster. When I reached her, I changed her diaper and then settled into the rocker in the corner. Her mouth opened as her hands reached for the bottle. As I rocked, I held her close; she smelled like Blake. His cologne must have rubbed off on her sleeper when he was holding her earlier. I closed my eyes and pictured the two of them in the family room. He was so good with her, and it made my heart swell.

oooooooooo

Blake

I felt like a teenager again every time I thought about Brooke. I don't know what it was, but just being around her was enough at times. I meant it when I told her I'd be back today.

I grabbed two blankets and a Thermos of coffee before rushing out of my apartment. I had the day off, and planned to spend as much of it as I could with her. I tossed the items in the back of my Audi, and drove to Emily's House. It wasn't that far, and when I got there I parked right in front on the street. I debated for a moment, but then decided to leave the car running as I rushed up the steps. I knocked quickly, looked around, and waited for the door to swing open. It was chilly out, but not too cold.

"Morning." Donna smiled when she answered the door. "Wanna come in?"

"I left the car running." I glanced over my shoulder, then back at Donna. "Can you let Brooke know that I'm here, and for her and Ava to dress warm?" I rubbed my hands together before stuffing them in my pockets.

"Brooke! Blake's here! Wear a coat!" she called over her shoulder before looking back at me and grinning.

"What's so funny?" I gave myself the once over before peering at my reflection in a nearby window. I looked ok. Nothing was out of place.

"Nothing," Donna mused. I hated when women did that; tell you it was nothing when it was most certainly something.

Before I could think too much about it, Brooke appeared behind Donna. She was holding Ava, and missing a coat. "Grab your coat. Get one for her too." I nodded at Ava. Brooke's forehead crinkled. "A car carrier for her too." I rocked back on my heels.

"I'm not big on surprises," Brooke mumbled.

"We're going for a drive. Not a surprise." I smiled. "Hurry up. Car's running." She disappeared for a moment, and then reappeared holding Ava's car seat. It had some fluffy cover over it that was zipped up under her chin. Brooke was wrapped in a winter coat and some Uggs.

"Is this ok?" She glanced from me to the ground as she motioned to herself.

"Perfect." I held out my hand and attempted to extract the baby carrier. "I can buckle this in." I smiled at her.

"Oh, ok." She released it, and followed me to the car. "Is this yours?" She opened the passenger door as I opened one of the back ones.

"Yeah. I don't drive much because I live close to the hospital." I clicked the seatbelt over Ava's carrier, tugged it to make sure it was snug, and then closed the door. "Hop in." I held her door as she slipped inside. After closing it, I jogged around to the driver's side.

"This is nice." She shivered against the cold as I put the car in drive.

"You haven't seen anything yet." I grinned as I pushed a few buttons to turn on her seat warmer. After a few moments, she shifted in her seat. "Feels good, right?" I glanced at her as I maneuvered through traffic.

"Un huh." She leaned back and sighed before turning to stare out the window. "Where are we going?"

"Not far," I mused. I know she said she didn't like surprises, but I didn't want to ruin what I had planned. "Just trust me, ok?" I looked over quickly, before making a turn to head out of town.

oooooooooo

Brooke

I didn't like surprises. I told him this, but he wouldn't give. My heart thundered in my chest as we drove farther away from town. Part of me was scared out of my mind. If something happened, I was too far away from anyone or anything that I knew. The other part of me said this was Blake, and he'd never hurt me. As much as I wanted to listen to that part, the scared part was winning. I just didn't know what to make of the situation. Ava was sound asleep in the backseat, completely oblivious to everything around her.

"We're almost there. I promise." Blake made another turn, this time onto a gravel drive. Signs for Macadown Beach appeared along the road as we bumped along.

"The beach?" I furrowed my brow as the road ended in a gravel parking area.

"I thought it would be nice to get away from the city for the day." Blake smiled and then his face fell in defeat. "Is this a bad idea?"

"No. I'm just surprised is all." I stared out the windshield at the gray sky. Gulls flew sporadically and waves crashed in the distance. It was a gloomy day for the beach. "It's kinda cold." I wrapped my arms around myself.

"I'll keep you warm." Blake pushed open his door, and climbed out. I sat there staring for a moment as he unbuckled Ava's carrier and came around to my door. He had blankets draped over one arm and Ava on the other. It was actually sweet the way he was trying to do everything.

He set the carrier down as he opened my door. "If you're not enjoying yourself within a few minutes, we can leave." His face looked sad, like he was disappointed in my reaction.

"It's not that I want to leave, I've just never had anyone do anything like this for me." I smiled as I stood up and pulled my coat tighter.

"It's empty this time of year. We'll have the beach to ourselves." Blake picked Ava back up, adjusted the items in his arms, and then reached for my hand. "Stop worrying for a day. Let me show you what life can be like. Just let go. I'll be your safety net."

The fear seemed to leave, but was replaced by something else… hope, maybe? My heart sped up as he helped me over the dunes and the sight before me took my breath away.

Chapter 16

Brooke

Blake had already been here. He'd planned this out. Sitting on the sand, a few feet in front of us was a plaid blanket. There was a basket in the middle holding it in place. He led me closer before setting Ava's carrier down on the corner beside him. When I gave him an odd look, he brushed me off.

"I'll watch her for now. She's sleeping, and this morning is about you." His head dipped as a smile started to form. "Hungry?" He opened the basket and started lifting things out. "I've got bagels, scones, and croissants. I wasn't sure what you'd like."

"A bagel is fine," I murmured. I'd never had a man prepare any breakfast of sorts.

"What do you really want, Brooke? Fine is not my goal here. I'm looking for 'great'." He laughed as he stared at me. "Take your time and think about it."

I pressed my lips together as thoughts of Warren floated through my head. He'd always criticized me when I ate. He'd tell me to eat less, or I'd get fat. He portioned my food when we were first married until he 'taught me' how to eat.

"Whatever you're thinking about, stop." He gently touched my arm. "What do you want to eat?"

I swallowed. "I'll take a little of each, please."

"I can do that." Blake chuckled as he lifted a paper plate out of the basket and began cutting the pastries in half. "Here ya go." He handed me the plate before reaching for a Styrofoam cup. "Coffee?" He opened the Thermos that he'd carried from the car, and poured hot liquid into the cup before handing it over.

"There's cream in this?" I was confused. He always drank his coffee black.

"That's the way you drink it, right?" He peeked in on Ava before looking back at me.

"Yes, but…" I pinched my mouth shut. I didn't want to ruin this.

"Stop," he repeated softly. "I'll tell you this as much as I need to. This is about you, not me." He pointed to himself. "I can drink it with cream, I just prefer not to."

I sipped the coffee. It felt good against the cold breeze coming off the water. The waves crashed in the distance, muffling the sound of my pounding heart. We sat there in silence munching away on our breakfast. We both had our knees bent as we stared at the sun trying to peek through the clouds. "I've always loved the beach." I sighed as I finished my bagel.

"Did you used to come here a lot?" Blake glanced at me.

"When I was a kid. Warren didn't like the sand, so we never came here," I grumbled.

"You didn't come by yourself?" Blake turned toward me slightly.

"Wasn't allowed to." I leaned forward and wrapped my arms around my knees. "I wasn't allowed to do a lot of things. Shopping for example. I wasn't allowed to go out shopping alone, only with him."

"Have you been out shopping since moving into the house?" He finished his breakfast, and placed the plate back in the basket.

"A few times." I smiled as I thought about the day Donna took me out to buy baby stuff. I hadn't really been out much since she'd been born.

"I have next Tuesday off. Would that work?" He thumbed through the calendar on his phone.

"What?" I was confused.

"I can babysit. You and one of the other ladies can have a girls day." He shrugged as if it was no big deal, but this was a very big deal to me.

"Um," I stammered. I was caught so off guard it wasn't even funny.

"Just think about it." He smiled as he tapped away on his phone. "I booked the time for you, so if you decide not to go, we can grab lunch or something."

"Ok," I mumbled as I twisted my hands together. I didn't know what to do at the moment. Ava was sleeping, we'd finished our food, and I was so out of my element.

"Relax." Blake rubbed my arm gently. "I can feel the tension all over you. This isn't a test here. I'm not trying to trick you, or catch you in any kind of trap. I'm trying to teach you. I want you to see that what you went through isn't normal. Are there bad men out there? Yes. I'm sure Warren's not the only one, but there are more of us 'good guys' than there are bad. I want to give you what he robbed you of. You're not going to upset me or offend me by reacting genuinely. If you don't like something, then tell me." His voice was soft, but held authority.

"I'm sorry." I sighed. "This is new, and you don't understand. He 'trained' me to react the way I do. It's going to take time and more than a few dates to undo the years of brainwashing I've had."

"You seem to be making good progress. Donna's got you recognizing that it was brainwashing." He picked at a thread on the blanket.

"Donna's been helping me with a lot. I've learned that I need to be patient and to listen to what my head is telling me. It might not make sense at the moment, but usually our instincts are right." I stared at the water. The push and pull of the waves reminded me of my thoughts. I felt like I was being pushed and pulled in a lot of different directions. I've learned to try and go with it for the most part. The crash of the waves was like the noise in my head. Every time I tried to make a decision about something there was always noise to go along with it. I've learned over the last couple of weeks how to turn that off, but sometimes the noise seems more powerful than me.

"What are you thinking about?" Blake nudged my shoulder. "I can see the wheels turning as we sit here."

"Not much," I murmured.

"Honesty, Brooke. Be honest with me. Don't worry about how I'll react. I'm not going to punish you like Warren did, no matter what." He turned slightly and tucked a hair behind my ear.

I took a big breath and closed my eyes before letting it out. "I was thinking about you, me, what we are, if I'm ready for that, if I even know what that is," I whispered. "If I want that." I swallowed against the idea. Did I want Blake to keep coming around? I enjoyed spending time with him, but did I want more? Could I handle more?

"I know you just got your papers yesterday, but you left your husband a long time ago." Blake reached over and placed his hand on top of mine. It was warm and strong. My pulse picked up more, and my breath caught. "When did you stop loving him?" He stared at my eyes for a moment before searching my face for truth.

"The first time he sent me to the hospital." Tears filled my eyes. "He got mad at me one night. He was late, and I ate without him. I'd left him food on a plate in the fridge. He came into the living room where I was watching TV and yanked me out of the chair by my arm so hard, he pulled my shoulder out of the socket, then he blamed me for letting it happen. I remember calling a cab because he wouldn't drive me to the ER, and I couldn't drive myself. I lied and told the intake nurse I'd fallen." I stared out at the waves. The sky was starting the darken, and it seemed to match my melancholy mood.

"You became property to him. Something to control. That's not love or marriage." Blake reached up and gently cupped my chin in his palm. He lightly turned my head until I was staring right into his eyes. "I would never want a woman as property. Marriage is a partnership. I want you to know that no matter what happens here, I will never ever inflict pain on you. Whether it's physical or mental, you will never be punished by me. When spouses disagree, they talk and work it out; nothing warrants any type of punishment." He leaned in and rested his forehead against mine. His breath feathered across my lips, and his nose brushed mine softly. We stayed there just soaking in the moment, eyes closed, listening to the waves crash in the distance. Our breathing increased the longer we stayed there. The tension rose, and I thought I may succumb to it and pull away, but I forced myself to let the moment play out. Just as the first snowflake fell, Blake's lips brushed across mine.

He started to pull back, but stopped himself, feathering them over mine once more. Within a moment his palm moved to my cheek, then neck as his lips parted and sealed more fully over mine. It was a kiss like no other, and despite how much it scared me, it thrilled me just the same. I hadn't been kissed like this in so long. Warren kissed me when we were first dating, but it quickly changed and became more of an obligation than romance. This, this was different. I could feel everything he was trying to tell me in that moment. The way he threaded his fingers in my hair, the way his lips moved, the way he sighed when he pulled away. It was as if he was telling me all the things he couldn't find words for, and I understood him.

"Was that ok?" He shifted on the blanket and smiled when a snowflake hit my nose.

"Yeah." I nodded. I wanted to say more, but I didn't have the words. How do you tell someone that they seem too perfect? How do you let yourself believe that reality really is real, and you're not dreaming? How do you let yourself love again?

"I think we better go before it starts coming down too hard. I don't want Ava to get too cold either." He tucked the blanket tighter around my sleeping daughter before standing and helping me up.

After walking us to the car, he ran back to grab the blankets and supplies. He smiled when he jumped in the driver's seat, and began our trek home. We didn't say anything. We just enjoyed being there together. It was like we knew what the other was thinking without needing the words. It was scary for me, but I knew deep down that Blake was someone worth taking a chance on. He was the one I'd been waiting for. I endured the pain to find him.

Chapter 17

Brooke

I spent most of yesterday analyzing everything that had happened at the beach with Blake. I went over it piece by piece, moment by moment, overthinking and judging everything. Did I say something wrong? Do something wrong? Did he mean what he said? Why hadn't I heard anything from him?

When I woke up this morning, the ground was covered in white. It looked beautiful outside, and I marveled at the scene from my window. Donna had left early to make sure she had time to get to work, and so had most of the girls. Ava had been sleeping better, and I felt like I actually got a good night's sleep from the night before with the exception of my brain constantly thinking about Blake. He'd left for a mid-day shift once he dropped me off, and I haven't seen or heard anything since. That fact alone is causing me to worry. The questions play on repeat in my head, and it seems that every time I start to feel better, they start back up again.

"Wanna get an up-close view?" Lauren called from my doorway.

"Up-close?" I stared at her blankly.

"Like go outside." She laughed. "You could put Ava in that carry thing, and we could walk the block. Just a thought." She turned to walk away, but I stopped her.

"Sure. Give me a few minutes." I glanced down at my leggings and then Ava's sleeper. I was still figuring out this whole 'how to dress the baby' thing. I grabbed the snow suit Donna had given me for Ava, and began putting it on her. She seemed to think it was a game. I'd pull one leg through, and while I was working on getting the second leg through, Ava would pull the first one back out. "What are you doing, silly girl?" I tickled her belly.

She laughed and flailed her arms and legs, causing the other leg to come out of the suit. "We're never going to get outside if you keep that up." I started over at least three times before I managed to get both legs to stay in, then I moved onto the arms, and that was just as difficult.

After getting Ava ready, I grabbed a pair of sweatpants to put on over my leggings. I'd always worn layers at home, so now shouldn't be any different. I pulled a hoodie on, and then grabbed my coat. As I made my way out to the living room with Ava, I felt like a penguin waddling. Lauren was sitting on the couch with her coat on.

"Want some help?" She stood and took the baby sling from me.

"Yes. It took me forever to get her in that thing." I sighed. Lauren strapped the sling around me, and held it in place while I threaded Ava's legs through.

"I think we're good." She smiled as she gave it a little tug to see if it was secure. "Let's go before we change our minds." She opened the door, and I knew what she meant in that exact moment.

As the door opened, we were blasted with freezing air. The temperature must have dropped at least twenty degrees since I was on the beach. "Crap! This is cold." I shivered as I held Ava closer. She was snuggled against me, and already sleeping.

"She doesn't seem too bothered by it." Lauren laughed as she pointed at Ava.

We made our way down the stairs and turned to walk along the sidewalk. It was a standard city block, and people were out shoveling the sidewalk. I had boots on, so the snow didn't really bother me.

"How was your date yesterday?" Lauren nudged my shoulder.

"Is that what this is? You wanna know about Blake?" I stopped and faced her.

Lauren giggled. "We all do. We've all met Dr. Blake at the hospital. He's never come to visit any of us, just you." She pointed at me.

"He took me to the beach. We had breakfast. That was it." I nibbled my lip nervously. I didn't want to talk about this. I didn't want to be house gossip.

"That's it? Are you two dating now?" I had sped up, and now she was matching my pace.

"I don't know. I'm not really ready to talk about it," I muttered.

"Fine, but I want to be the first to know." Lauren smiled as we turned the corner. We walked quietly together just watching the snow fall. It was like a Christmas card. Businesses were starting to decorate for the holidays, kids were building snowmen, and people were clearing their steps and porches. I'd almost forgotten where I was, I was so lost in the scenery.

"We need to move faster, Brooke." Lauren put her arm around me and started guiding me up the sidewalk.

"I don't want to slip. What's wrong?" I started looking around, but Lauren was blocking my view.

"Just trust me," she hissed. I forced us to stop moving before I stepped away from her to look around. It was then that I saw him. Right across the street and standing at the crosswalk, was Warren. His head was covered in a black beanie and he was wearing a long, dark wool coat. His eyes bore into mine as the 'don't walk' sign changed to 'walk'. As I stood there rooted to my spot, Warren's long legs began to eat up the pavement. Lauren tugged at my arm, but it was like I was frozen in place. I couldn't move, I couldn't make myself do anything but wait. All the therapy I'd been going to had still not broken Warren's training. He'd always told me running was worse. If I ran from him, my punishment would be worse. I'd trained myself to stand still when I saw him; to not move, and in this moment my body was doing just that. "Come on." Lauren pulled again, but I didn't budge.

She stayed there with me, I don't know why, until Warren made it to our side of the crosswalk. He gave me a disapproving smile as his eyes scanned over me. "I thought I taught you better. I can't believe you came outside dressed like that," he scoffed as my eyes went downcast. I knew better than to look him in the eyes.

"You're not supposed to be here," I mumbled.

"I can be wherever I want." He sneered as his arm raised toward me.

I stepped back, and instinctively wrapped my arms around Ava. "You can't be here," I mumbled again. I glanced at Lauren and noticed she had her phone out and was furiously typing a text.

"You need to leave," she growled at Warren. "I've called the police. They'll be here any minute."

"This is none of your concern," he snapped at her before redirecting his attention to me. "You've turned into quite the little slut lately, haven't you? Prancing around with that doctor. You think he sees anything different than I do? You're stupider than I thought. He sees a pair of legs, that's it." Warren threw his head back and laughed. "He's in for a rude awakening if he thinks that he's getting in there. Hell, I couldn't get there without force. I don't know what you're trying to prove with all this," he waved his arms around, "but you're fooling yourself if you think you'll make it. You'll be on my steps begging me to take you back in a few months. You're too dumb to survive on your own."

As I stood there in shock, letting his words hit their mark, he turned and almost jogged down the block. It was then that I looked up to see flashing lights of a patrol car rounding the corner. Lauren stepped closer, and attempted to put her arm around me. "Let's go back," she murmured, but I shook her off.

"You go back. I need to stay." The snow was falling heavier at this point and I was freezing, but Warren's words were all I could think about. Was he right about Blake? Was Blake using me? Would he want me if he knew all the things Warren did?

"Everything ok?" Cal's voice broke me out of my trance as he stepped from his patrol car by the curb.

"I think she's in shock." Lauren's eyes went from me to Cal.

"I got it." Cal moved closer. "You head back. I'll make sure she gets back ok." Lauren nodded and started walking briskly the rest of the way around the block. "Brooke?" He held his hand out as he approached. It was then that I realized I was just standing there in the middle of the sidewalk, not moving.

"No." I shook my head. "I don't think I can do this," I murmured.

"Do what?" Cal moved me toward his car.

"Live…love…survive?" I shrugged as if all those things were suddenly a question.

"Yes, you can. Don't let him get to you. He's trying to break you. You're stronger than that. I know you." Cal carefully put me in the car. "I'm gonna drive you home." He climbed in and maneuvered us around to the house.

After helping me up the front steps, he pulled out a form. "I need you to sign this." He handed it over.

"What is it?" I stared at the black and white print in front of me.

"You're pressing charges. He violated the OP, that means you can press charges. Since it's only the second time, I don't know what they'll do, but if he keeps doing it he can be locked up." I blindly signed the paper, just going through the motions of being told what to do. "I'm going to check on you after my shift." Cal folded the paper and put it back in his pocket.

"Ok." I waved him off, turned, and trudged up to my room. Ava was still sleeping against me, and I felt like I needed a nap too. How had this day gone so bad, so fast?

Chapter 18

Brooke

I don't know how long I slept, it felt like most of the day. When I woke up, it was starting to get dark. The sun was setting, and the snow had stopped falling. "You plan on joining us for dinner?" Donna knocked softly on my door.

"Yeah." I yawned as I sat up. I glanced over at where Ava was lying in her bed. She was awake, but happy. I lifted her up, and smiled as she kicked her feet. "You're a happy girl, aren't you?" Ava blinked a few times as her mouth curved into a smile. "We'll be there as soon as I change her." I glanced at Donna as I laid Ava on the bed.

"Ok. See you in a few." Donna turned and left. She hadn't said much since Cal brought me back, and I've been keeping to myself most of the day.

I tickled Ava's belly as I unsnapped her onesie, carefully going through the steps of changing her. After snapping her back up, I grabbed a clean bottle and made my way to the kitchen.

Donna and Amy were bustling about, bringing food to the table. Lauren had gone to work, and the others weren't home yet. "Anything I can help with?" I murmured as I began scooping formula into the bottle.

"I think we've just about got it. Go ahead and feed her, and then we'll join you." Amy smiled.

I carried Ava into the dining room and sat down. As much as I wanted to be my usual self, I felt like I was just going through the motions. I was numb, plain and simple. One run in with Warren and I was back to where I'd been months before. How was I ever going to change if I couldn't get past something like this?

ooooooooo

Blake

I'd worked a double shift today so I could have tomorrow off. I'd been wanting to spend the day with Brooke. Christmas was just around the corner, and I knew Donna didn't have a tree yet. I asked Dan, the head of my department, if I could switch shifts with him. I hated the doubles, but it meant I could take Brooke out tree shopping.

I was just walking to my car when my brother came jogging up the sidewalk. His hat was pulled down over his ears, and his breath was coming out in puffs as if he'd been running. "Hang on!" He threw his hands in the air to stop me. I froze where I was, and let my shoulders sag. I was tired. I needed sleep, and talking to him was the last thing I wanted to do. When he caught up to me, he bent over and placed his hands on his thighs. "Did she tell you?" he puffed.

"Who? Tell me what?" I wiped my palm down my face.

"Brooke." He gave me a duh look. "That asshole ex approached her today."

"What?" I turned to face him, fists clenched at my sides.

"She went for a walk with one of the other girls, and he crossed the street and cornered her. Luckily her friend called the police," Cal growled.

"I haven't heard anything from her since we went to the beach. I was trying to give her time. After the kiss…" I trailed off.

"Wait! You kissed her?" His head whipped around, and he blinked a few times.

"Yeah. It was nothing big; I mean for her it probably was, but it was one kiss. Wait. Tell me more about having to come save her. Did he touch her?" I started pacing the sidewalk. It was freezing out, but I wasn't feeling the cold at the moment.

"No, at least I don't think so. She had the baby with her. By the time I got there, they were just standing there. He was saying something that made her uncomfortable. The look on her face said she was terrified. He wasn't touching her in any way, but he had total control over her. I think she would have gone with him if I wasn't there. It was like she was on autopilot." Cal sighed. "I've seen this before. Some are so broken they have a hard time making decisions and thinking for themselves."

"I gotta go." I started running toward my car. The wind whipped around me, cutting through my scrubs as if they were made of cheese cloth.

After scraping the ice off the windshield, I cranked the engine and tapped my foot, waiting for the heat to kick in. As my seat warmed, I relaxed slightly and carefully pulled out of my parking space. I probably should have driven a little slower, but the anger boiling in my gut wouldn't let me.

oooooooooo

It didn't take long to get to Emily's House, and I parked right on the street out front. The porch was only lit by a single light, and the steps were shoveled off. I jogged up, and knocked on the door with more force than I should have.

"Just a minute," came a voice from somewhere inside. Amy's head peeked out around the door. "Oh, hey." She opened the door wider. "Come in. It's freezing out there." She stepped back and let me pass.

As I stepped inside, I knocked my shoes on the threshold to bang off as much snow as possible. "Is Brooke here?" I glanced around.

"She's in her room." Amy motioned to the hallway. Donna was sitting in a chair reading, and smiled slightly as I made my way toward the hall.

"She's not herself tonight," Donna warned.

"Thanks." I waved her off. I was half angry and half concerned. Why hadn't she called me? Why was I finding this out from my brother?

ooooooooo

"Brooke?" I knocked on the half-closed door. I knew Ava would be in there, and I wasn't sure if she was sleeping. "It's Blake." I waited for an answer, but nothing came. "I'm coming in," I warned as I pushed the door open. As the door slowly creaked open, Brooke's still form appeared on the bed. Ava was in her crib cooing at the mobile spinning above her. "Brooke?" I tried again as I stepped over the threshold. "Cal told me what happened." The closer I moved to her, the more the anger I was feeling dissipated. I was more hurt now than anything. "Brooke?" She still wouldn't acknowledge me as I carefully lowered myself onto the edge of her bed. There were no lights on in the room. The only light was coming from the street lights and the moon. Her face glistened in the street light from where tears had tracked down her cheeks.

"Brooke?" I placed my palm on her shoulder. "Talk to me," I begged.

"Why?" It was the first word to fall from her lips, and as much as I knew whatever she was about to say would hurt, I couldn't stop begging her to open up. "I'm broken, and hopeless, and not worth whatever this is." She flicked her hand between us before rolling away from me.

"That's not true," I whispered. I swallowed the lump in my throat as I slipped out of my coat, and tossed it toward a chair in the corner. I toed off my boots and then scooted closer to her. "You are not broken. He didn't break you. You're strong. You're stronger than you'll ever know."

"Sure, I am," she muttered. "You're wasting your time with me." Her voice choked up as she curled into a tighter ball.

"No, I'm not. You're a great person, Brooke, and a great mom. He can't hurt you anymore." I moved closer and attempted to pull her toward me. I just wanted to wrap her in my arms at this point.

I glanced over, and noticed Ava had fallen asleep. "I don't want to wake Ava, but I want to hold you. I think you need that, and I think you need to let out whatever you're holding in right now." I moved closer, and laid down beside her. "Brooke?" I tugged her shoulders and this time she rolled toward me. Her tearstained face was shadowed by the darkness, but I could see the pain and uncertainty. "Come here." I opened my arms, and she collapsed on my chest. Her face nuzzled into the crook of my neck, and her arms curled against my chest. Her body shuddered as her tears came back.

"I don't know how to do this," she whimpered as I stroked her back.

"Every day is a learning experience, and I'll do whatever I can to help you. He took years to do this to you. You can't expect to fix it in just a few weeks. It's gonna take time." I tightened my grip as she struggled to get closer.

"Please don't let go." Her voice sounded as if she was begging.

"I won't. I won't ever let go," I promised, and it was the first time that all this felt real. I knew there was something here, but I don't think I realized it went as deep as it does until this moment.

I laid there for hours, staring at the ceiling of her room while she slept against me. Ava never woke up, and Brooke seemed to finally get some peace. I think I might have drifted off sometime after midnight. I don't really know. I do know that it was one of the best night's sleep I've gotten in a long time.

I left Emily's House around six the next morning. I awoke with the sunrise. Brooke and Ava were still fast asleep. I carefully slipped from her bed, grabbed my things, and tiptoed out to the living area. Donna was reading the morning paper and sipping coffee.

"I'll tell her you had to leave." Donna smirked as she took a sip from her mug.

"I'm coming back. We're going to get a tree for in here today. I need to shower though. I worked a double before I came over here." I yawned.

"Mmmhmm." Donna nodded. "You don't need to explain anything to me. I knew she was special the first night you treated her in the ER. You had that look."

"I don't have a look." I scowled.

"You do with her. She's gonna take a lot of time and patience. I hope you can handle that," she warned.

"I'm not going anywhere. I'm not letting go so easy with her." I pointed at the hallway. "See you later. I need to get this hospital smell off me." The truth was, I smelled like Brooke, and I needed to get home and take care of business before Donna saw just how much I liked her.

"You wanna leave a note?" Donna mused.

"Just tell her to dress warm, and I'll be back around lunchtime." I waved as I opened the front door to make my way over to my snow-covered car. We were getting a tree, and decorating it tonight. It was time I gave Brooke some memories to replace the ones that were currently filling her head.

Chapter 19

Blake

After cleaning up at home and putting on some warmer clothes, I called my brother. I wanted to borrow his truck, and see where things were going with Warren's arrest. I didn't get very far. He got all professional on me and told me he couldn't discuss the case. I wasn't part of it, so I didn't have any right to know what was going on. He did leave his keys for me at the front desk in the station.

I was currently walking to the station. The snow was picking up again, and I didn't want to risk ending up in the ditch or worse, plowing into another car. After grabbing the keys, I found the truck parked on the street a few spaces away. I climbed in, and turned the heat all the way up. It was cold today, and the sun was hiding.

I drove to pick up Brooke, and was surprised to find her waiting on the porch when I got there. I pulled up to the curb, and left the truck running while I hopped out. "It's freezing! Why didn't you wait inside?" I jogged toward the steps and almost wiped out on a patch of ice.

"It's slippery out." Brooke's eyes went wide. "Be careful."

"I can see that." I cringed as I reached the steps. When I got to the top, I really looked at her. She looked beautiful sitting there on the porch swing. She was wearing a pair of dark jeans that tucked into her boots. Her purple coat was zipped up with a big pink scarf wrapped around her neck. It was partially covering her mouth. Her brown hair was pulled back loosely and a matching pink hat was tugged down over her ears. Her cheeks and nose were pink from the cold, and her arms were wrapped around herself. "I would've come in. You don't have to wait outside for me." I softened my voice.

"I know, but I wanted some fresh air. This seemed safe." She shrugged.

"Where's Ava?" I glanced around. Brooke has always been a very attentive mother. It surprised me that Ava wasn't close by.

"Donna's watching her. She said she missed spending time with her, and for me to enjoy myself today." A small smile curved at the corner of her lips peeking out from the scarf.

"Well, if you're ready, let's get in the truck. It's cold." I shivered against the wind as I led her down to the passenger side.

"You have a truck too?" Her brow crinkled in confusion.

"It's Cal's. He owes me." I chuckled.

"Where are we going?" She buckled her seat belt as I closed the door. I held up a finger as I jogged around to the driver's side, almost falling on the ice once again.

"I thought we could grab some breakfast, and then we're tree shopping." I grinned.

"Tree shopping?" Her head jerked back.

"For a Christmas tree. There's a lot just outside of town that always has nice trees. I thought we could pick one out for the house and decorate it tonight." I pulled away from the curb and started heading to the diner I frequented sometimes.

"We never had a live tree, only artificial ones. Live ones drop a lot of needles." Her face twisted as she said the words.

"Do you like the artificial ones better?" She was revealing more of her past, and I wanted to keep her talking, but I knew it must have been a painful memory.

"I don't know." She seemed confused. "I've never had a live one to compare it to. Maybe this is a good idea." She bounced a little in her seat like she was having a revelation.

"Live tree it is then." I laughed as I pulled into the parking lot of Fran's Diner.

"Wait!" Brooke's eyes darted around. "I've been here, I think." She blinked a few times as she rubbed her temples.

"This place has been here forever. It wouldn't surprise me if you had." I attempted to soothe her.

"But I walked here; from my house; with Ava." She shook her head and rubbed her temples again. "Maybe I haven't been here; that didn't make sense." She released a frustrated sigh as she leaned back against the seat.

"It's ok if you haven't. We can try something new." I smiled as I cut the engine and climbed out. After helping her out of the truck, we walked inside. "Wanna sit at the counter?" I motioned to some stools.

"Sure." She had a tormented look on her face as we made our way to the stools and sat down.

It didn't take long for a server to stop in front of us. "What can I get you?" She stood poised to take our order, but Brooke just stared off in the distance.

"We'll take two specials and coffee." I smiled and then reached over and rubbed my palm up and down Brooke's back. She seemed so lost at the moment.

oooooooo

Brooke

Everything looked the same. The counter was the same; the stools; all the décor; it was all the same. The menu and the staff looked the same. I don't ever remember coming here with Warren, and the fact that the diner was here, and not in my town was confusing. Was this place real?

I could hear Blake ordering food for us, but I just stared through the opening to the kitchen. Ava and I used to watch the cook make pancakes at my Fran's. We'd sit here and watch as we drank our shakes after I picked her up from school. I couldn't help but stare as the cook moved around, unknowingly giving me a headache.

"Are you ok?" Blake whispered as he leaned closer. "Was this a bad choice?"

"I'm fine," I murmured as I twisted my hands together in my lap. "I'm just having a déjà vu moment. I'll be fine." I brushed him off. How could I tell him that I've been here, but I haven't been here? How would he ever understand? I don't even understand.

"Are you sure?" he pressed on as the waitress poured two coffees in front of us.

"Yes." I nodded. I knew I couldn't tell him that I was freaking out on the inside. I'd sound crazy. I reached to the left without even looking and my fingers wrapped around the container of sugar. As I poured some into my coffee, my vision went blurry. The room started spinning, and I knew I needed to get away. I need to process what was happening. "I'll be right back," I mumbled as I stood and turned in the direction of the bathroom.

"Ok." Blake sounded confused, but I didn't have time to check. I walked as fast as I could to the back corner. I knew the bathroom was there. It was there in my dreams. When I saw the door, my head spun a little more. I'd never been here. What was happening? My breathing picked up as I shoved at the door, and stepped inside.

I placed my hands on the counter by the sink and leaned forward, letting my head drop. I took a few deep breaths before glancing at my reflection in the mirror. The bathroom had red tile. The one in my dream was black. The red glared back at me, mocking me. It was proving that my dream wasn't real. "Get it together," I whispered to myself. I turned the cold water on, and splashed my face a little. The cold helped with my little breakdown as I took more deep breaths. I told myself more than once that this was real, and my dream wasn't, but for some reason my head didn't want to listen. I washed my hands, and then turned to go back to my spot at the counter.

"Everything all right?" Blake smiled as I sat back down.

"Un huh." I swallowed as I reached for the coffee. Within a few moments, our breakfast arrived.

"I wasn't sure what you'd want, so I ordered you the special." He offered me a napkin from the dispenser in front of him.

"This is fine." I offered a tight smile as I poured syrup over my pancakes. To avoid having to explain myself anymore, I cut off a bite and shoveled it into my mouth. Blake seemed to understand because he too started eating and all conversation dropped. There were so many questions floating around in my head, but I wasn't sure I wanted the answer to them. I knew one thing; I couldn't ask Blake. I was becoming too attached to him and couldn't do anything that might make him want to leave. I was falling fast and hard, and that part scared the crap outta me.

Chapter 20

Brooke

We didn't really talk during our meal. The sizzle of the flat top grill, and the ringing of the bell over the door filled the silence. There was a low hum of conversation that filled the diner, and at times it almost drowned out the rambling going on in my head.

When we finished, Blake paid, and held out his arm for me to head to the door. "Are you sure you're ok?" he whispered in my ear. "You've been really quiet since we got here. Did Warren bring you here or something?" His eyes softened as he held open the door and we stepped out onto the sidewalk. He led us toward the truck, and I fought to figure out how to explain this.

"It's not you, it's me," I growled in frustration. "I know that's a lame excuse. Warren never brought me here. As far as I know, I've never eaten here. It's just…" I sighed.

"What? You can talk to me," he coaxed as he opened my door. I climbed in, he shut the door, and rushed around to his side.

As he shut his door and cranked the engine, I closed my eyes and pictured my town. "Have you ever had a dream that seemed real? I don't mean like it could happen, but one where you believed it did happen?"

"Sure, I guess." Blake let the truck idle, and turned to face me more.

"I don't know when all of this happened, or how long it took." I shook my head as images of the white farm house came flitting through my head. The beach, Ava's first Christmas, the tree house, Officer Blake, all the home repairs, it was endless. "The first time we met, in the hospital, wasn't the first time for me. While I was unconscious, I ran away from Warren. I had Ava, and we ran. We ran all over the country. When we found safety, it was in a little country town. You were there, but you were a cop. You fixed my house. You built stuff for Ava. You wanted to be our friend. We walked everywhere, and there was a diner in town. It was called Fran's Diner, and it looked just like this one only different colors." I turned to stare out the window. "I get it if you think I'm crazy. I would too."

"I don't think you're crazy." His voice was soft.

I turned to face him, "You don't?"

"I think you're amazing. You had a brain injury. It's common for parts of the brain to not remember trauma. It's also normal for an injured brain to come up with its own reality. There's nothing happening right now that's not normal. I promise." He cupped my cheek. "You're talking about my job. I study the brain, and yours has been through a lot." He leaned closer. "Please don't ever feel like you can't tell me something."

"Ok." I let my gaze dip. "I think you're pretty amazing too," I murmured as I refused to look up.

I heard him swallow. I heard him shift in the seat. I heard every movement that happened over the next few seconds. It was a memory that I'd hold onto for years to come. Aside from our morning on the beach, this was the next most important moment. Blake leaned forward and pressed his lips to mine. This wasn't the sweet innocent kiss we shared on the beach. This was Blake kissing my soul. His head tipped to the side as his tongue ran across the seam of my lips. I let him in. I let him in willingly as I sighed and leaned closer. It was like my body knew exactly what it wanted, and it wanted Blake.

We moved closer as his fingers threaded in the hair on the back of my head. I braced myself on the seat as I leaned in. His tongue licked at the inside of my mouth softly, swiping and exploring. He was nothing like Warren. Warren was all business and never romance. Blake was showing me that I was in control. He never pushed further; never tried to touch me. He groaned as I pressed myself against his chest, looping my arms around his neck. We stayed locked like that, just softly exploring one another's mouths until finally he pulled back. "I need to stop while I still can," he mumbled as he righted himself in his seat. "Let's go get that tree before I change my mind."

"Sure." I smiled.

"God, you're beautiful. I don't even think you know how beautiful, and that makes it even more dangerous," he growled as he shifted the truck in drive and pulled out onto the road.

oooooooo

Blake

As I drove out of town, I kept glancing over at her. I tried to take as many peeks as I could without her noticing. I didn't want to scare her, but I couldn't help myself. There was still a blush on her cheeks from our kiss, and every once in a while, she'd get this far away look. I wondered if she was thinking of me like I was of her.

It didn't take us long to reach the tree lot. It was a small lot in front of a local farm that was right outside the city limits. It was one of those places that you'd drive right by if you didn't know about it. "We're here." I smiled as I made the final turn into the gravel parking lot. There was a tractor parked off to the side of the freshly plowed driveway and lot.

"Carson's Tree Farm. I've never heard of this place." Brooke leaned forward and read the name off the sign a few feet away.

"I've been getting Donna's trees here for the last few years. Old man Carson was happy to donate one when he found out what Donna was doing for everyone at the house." I climbed out of the truck, and pulled my coat tighter around me. The wind was blowing snow, and the ground was slippery. I made my way to Brooke's door, helped her out, and then led her over to where the trees were. "We get our pick of any of these with a red tag." I pointed to a row near the back. They were all around eight feet tall.

"Will this fit in the house?" Brooke tipped her head back to look up at the tree. Snow started falling again and began landing on her eyelashes.

"Sure." I laughed. "The house has ten-foot ceilings."

"Oh." Her mouth formed a little O and she looked slightly embarrassed.

"Which one do you like?" I motioned to several in front of us.

"This one has a nice shape." She smiled as she reached out and ran her fingers down one of the branches. She drew her hand back quickly. "That one pricked me."

"That is the difference between real and fake." I couldn't help but grin. "Does this mean you don't like the real ones?"

"They smell good." She leaned closer to the tree.

"Just wait until we get this in the house. The whole house will smell like it." I waved to one of the farmhands who was standing a little ways away. "We'll take this one." I pointed to the tree Brooke had picked out.

He nodded as he moved close. "Would you like it wrapped?"

"Yes." I reached for Brooke's hand and started leading her over to where we parked.

"Wrapped?" Her nose scrunched up.

"They put netting around it. It makes it easier to carry and get in the house." I pointed to the machine that our tree was currently being shoved through.

"Oh. That makes sense." She nodded before glancing at the truck. "Won't the needles scratch up your brother's truck?"

"Nah, and if they do, he owes me." I laughed as she frowned. "Something wrong?" I was confused. Why would she care about me scratching Cal's truck?

"No, it's just that he was nice to let you use it. I wouldn't want to mess it up or anything." She shrugged.

"Cal has broken plenty of things that were mine. I'm not worried." I chuckled as the farmhand tossed the tree in the back, and I helped Brooke back inside.

"I'm gonna drop you and the tree off at the house, and then I'm going to take Cal's truck back. After I drop it off, I'll be back to help with the tree." I pulled back into traffic and headed toward Emily's House.

"Ok." Brooke's voice was quiet as she stared out the window. I wasn't sure if something was wrong, but I wasn't going to ask now. I knew it had been a crazy day for her, and I didn't want to add to it. We'd talk tonight after we decorated the tree, and I'd find out what was up then.

ooooooo

When we arrived at the house, one of the girls was sitting on the porch much like Brooke was the first time I arrived. She waved as I parked on the street and left the truck running. I waved back as I helped Brooke out. "I'll be back in a bit. I'm going to stand the tree up on the porch. Donna can show you where the decorations are, and you guys can get them ready. Ok?" I bent my knees so I could look directly in her eyes. She smiled and nodded as she pressed her lips together. "Ok. Give me an hour, then I'm all yours."

As she walked up the steps, I grabbed the tree and carried it on my shoulder up to the porch. I propped it up against the house, and turned to head back to the truck. Just as I was pulling away from the curb, Brooke turned at the front door and waved. She was chatting with the other girl, and I could only imagine what they were talking about. I'd hoped it was something happy. Brooke laughed and then glanced back at me and it looked as if she was blushing again. Part of me hoped she was reliving our kiss, but the other part of me was just happy to see her smile. As much pain as she'd endured over the course of the last several years, she deserved to be happy. I only hoped that I could one day be the source of that happiness.

Chapter 21

Brooke

When Blake dropped me off at the house this afternoon, Amy was waiting on the porch. As soon as I climbed the steps, she jumped up and began firing questions at me. "Are you two dating? Where did you go? What's he really like? Has he kissed you yet?" She grinned at me, bouncing on her toes as she clasped her hands in front of her. You would think she was a teenager, not a woman in her late twenties.

I laughed as I waved at Blake pulling away from the curb. I could feel my face heating, and I wanted to get inside before he noticed. "Can we go in? It's cold out here." I shivered as I pulled the front door open.

"I guess." Amy shrugged. "You aren't getting off the hook that easy though." She giggled and I turned to look back at Blake. He was down the road a bit, but I could still see the lights of the truck. "There is so something going on with you two." She knocked my shoulder before I stepped through the door, and I knew she wasn't letting this go until I told her something.

Once inside, I hung up my coat and scarf, and put my boots away. I was doing anything and everything to avoid Amy's interrogation. When I stepped around the corner from the coat closet, Amy was standing there with her arms across her chest and tapping her foot. "What?" I shrugged.

"Could you take any longer?" She rolled her eyes. "I need to know what he's like when he's out on a date. I haven't been on a date in years, not a real one. My ex won't leave me alone long enough to have any kind of relationship." She sighed.

"I don't know if we're dating. I mean, we've been hanging out. He says he wants more, but I don't know what I want." I shuffled over to the couch and sat down.

"Do you like hanging out with him?" Amy touched my knee.

"Sure. He's sweet, and kind, and patient. I like the way he makes me feel." I smiled dreamily as I thought about our morning on the beach, and then breakfast at the diner. The fact that he didn't flip out when I told him about my dream was good too. "We've kissed…twice." My face heated. I could feel my heart starting to race and my neck heating too.

"A real one?" Amy grinned as she leaned closer. I felt like a preteen sharing secrets with my best friend.

"There are fake ones?" I twisted my face in confusion. "How do you fake a kiss?"

"No." She laughed. "I mean was it like the way your grandma would kiss you, or was it a kiss kiss." She leaned back and stared at me, her eyes darting around my face in the process. "Oh," she laughed. "I can tell by your face that it was a kiss kiss. Is he any good at it?" Her eyes widened.

"It was a kiss." I tried really hard to down play it. I was never the girl who talked about her boyfriends with her friends. I kept things to myself.

"Your face says it was a good kiss. I'm so happy for you." She leaned forward and wrapped me in a hug. "Good for you."

"Thanks… I think." I wrinkled my forehead.

"No thanks necessary, now let's get the decorations down before he comes back." She jumped up and clapped her hands together.

ooooooooo

Blake arrived right before dinner. Donna had made homemade bread and tomato soup. It tasted delicious on a cold night. Amy had started a fire in the fireplace, and Blake was currently trying to get the tree in the tree stand.

"Maybe if you turn it a little this way." Donna pointed to the right, and Blake twisted the tree.

"Now it's leaning toward me." Lauren frowned.

"How about we turn it this way?" Amy pointed toward the door, and Blake laughed.

"How about I tighten the stand first and we see where it leans naturally?" He sat down on the floor, and reached under the tree. "Everybody back up," he warned as he slowly let go. "I don't want this to fall on any of you." The tree leaned to the left slightly, and he pushed it back up and tightened that side of the stand. "This might be it." He released it again and backed up. The tree wobbled a bit at first, but then settled.

"Yay. You did it." Amy bounced on her toes as she skipped over to where the box of lights was sitting on the loveseat. "Why don't you help with these?" She handed me a strand. "Blake can do the top ones since he can reach." She grinned and then winked at me.

"O- ok," I stuttered as I stood and made way over toward him.

He smiled as he took an end of a strand. "Just follow me around the tree while I clip them on." We made quick work of it, and soon the tree was lit up with beautiful colors. They flashed and blinked, turning the room into sort of a disco.

"It's so pretty," Amy mused from where she was standing across the room. "Let's put the ornaments on." She handed each of us a box, and we carefully began unwrapping them, and hanging them on the tree.

"You guys did a great job picking this one out." Donna smiled as she stood back to look at the finished product. "It looks beautiful."

"It does," Blake murmured. I couldn't help but feel his eyes on me. When I glanced to the side, he was staring right at me.

"Anyone up for hot chocolate?" Donna clapped her hands.

"Ooh, me." Amy darted toward the kitchen.

"I think I'm going to bed. I have to be up early tomorrow for an appointment." Lauren stretched and then headed for the hallway.

"I'm just going to sit here for a while." I sat down on the couch and just stared at the tree. It was so pretty. I don't ever remember having a tree look as magical as this one. The lights twinkled and made the glass of some of the ornaments sparkle. Warren would have never been ok with this. Nothing matched. All our trees had a theme and everything matched.

ooooooo

"Mind if I join you?" Blake slowly lowered himself onto the couch beside me.

147

"Not at all." I scooted over to make room. "It's really pretty. It's nice of you to help Donna like this."

"I enjoy helping, and there's a perk this year… you're here." He winked as he leaned back and draped his arm over the back of the couch.

"I'm not that special," I mumbled. I wasn't used to the compliments, and Blake seemed to give them constantly.

"You are to me." He smiled softly as he shifted closer. The arm that was on the back of the couch slid forward to rest on my shoulders. He tugged gently, causing me to lean against him. As my side rested against his chest, I could feel his heartbeat. His breathing picked up, and he swallowed a few times before he started talking again. "I know you haven't heard this enough, but you are special, Brooke and I'm going to keep telling you that until you start believing it."

"You might have to say it a lot then." I sighed. I could feel tears coming, but I forced them back. I didn't want to ruin the moment.

"What's wrong?" Blake shifted slightly and pulled me closer. He was now leaning back, kinda half on and half off the couch. Both arms were wrapped around me in a hug, and I was leaning against his chest.

"Nothing. I was just thinking," I murmured.

"About what?" He started rubbing my back.

"About how pretty this tree is. About how something as simple as a pretty tree is something I've never had. About how if I'd decorated a tree like this, I would have been punished." I swallowed as memories flooded me.

"Why would you be punished for a tree?" Blake's voice changed from soothing to utterly confused.

"Everything had to match. There had to be order. You know the trees you see in department stores? The ones that have a theme, and the ornaments are all strategically placed? That's what our trees looked like." My voice had gone from happy to robotic with just a simple memory.

"That's crazy. Those trees are nice, but so is this kind. All the ornaments on this tree are handmade. The women who have stayed here over the years have made all of them. I'm sure Donna will have a craft day pretty soon so you can add to it."

"I remember this one year Warren wanted to decorate the entire house in blue, white, and silver. It was supposed to be a winter wonderland. I didn't have the correct ratio on the colors for the tree, and I put an angel on the top instead of a star. Warren knocked the tree down, shattering half the ornaments, and then shoved me on top of the wreckage. Not only did I get cuts all over me, but I had to clean up the mess." I didn't even realize I was crying at this point.

"What an asshole," Blake growled. "There's a special place for men like him."

"It's hard for me to look at things like this tree, and not pick apart what's wrong with it. Warren's made me think like him. I'm trying to see the beauty in things though, and tonight I do with this, so thank you." I turned to face him, my hands folded together on his chest.

"Thank me?" He pointed to himself. "What did I do?"

"You made me see this tree differently. I don't really know how, but seeing the joy you had while decorating it made me see the simple beauty. I'm making progress. I'll get there." I offered a half smile.

"God, you're beautiful." He sighed as he lifted his head and craned his neck to get closer. "I don't think you even know how beautiful you are, and how beautiful what you just said is."

When his lips touched mine, I sighed with acceptance. I was expecting it this time, and let myself enjoy it for what it was, a kiss. A kiss from someone who really seemed to care. A kiss that wasn't given with the expectation of more.

We laid there in each other's arms in the quiet of the night with only the tree lights and fire illuminating the room. The fire crackled and spread its warmth throughout the room. I don't remember when we fell asleep, but I know it was the first night I didn't dream of Warren. He didn't invade my dreams, he wasn't torturing me, I wasn't afraid. Blake made me feel safe and loved; he was showing me what I had deserved all along and it was this night that seemed to change things for us.

Chapter 22

Brooke

"Brooke," Blake's whispered voice invaded my sleep, "Brooke." It was more insistent this time, and came with a slight shake. "Ava's crying."

My eyes sprang open as I stretched. "I'm awake. I'm sorry." I scrambled to get up. My limbs were tangled with Blake's and there was a blanket over us. Did we sleep all night here?

"It's ok, she just started." He yawned as a goofy grin began to pull at his lips.

"What?" I glanced down at my skewed clothes.

"You're cute in the morning. I should have woken you the last time." He chuckled lightly.

I shook my head at him before rushing away to get Ava. I'm sure she was hungry and probably wet too. "Hey, pretty girl," I cooed as I lifted her out of her crib. She kicked her feet and smiled at me, all tears stopping the moment she saw me. "You ready for breakfast?" She smiled and opened her mouth as if she was trying to suck on something. "Let's get this wet diaper off, and then we'll get a bottle."

I laid her on the bed, and quickly changed her while listening to her attempt to talk to me. She was getting bigger now, and doing more than just sleeping and eating. She had good head control, and was trying to babble. There were some days I'd just lie on the bed with her, and pretend to have a conversation with her.

"Everything ok?" Blake's head peeked around the door. His hair was sticking up, and his bare feet were peeking out from under the legs of his jeans. He shifted back and forth like he was waiting for an invite.

"She's fine." I smiled. "Just wet and hungry." I snapped up her pjs and lifted her in my arms. "Let me get a bottle and I'll meet you back in the living room."

After mixing a bottle, I settled into the recliner in the living room. Blake was in the process of putting on his shoes. He sat up and glanced over at me before attempting to straighten his clothes. "She loves her bottles, huh?" He laughed lightly.

"When she first wakes up, yes." I grinned at Ava. "You're hungry in the morning, huh pretty girl?" Ava smiled around the nipple and kicked her feet.

"I was wondering if you and Ava would want to come over for dinner tonight?" Blake fidgeted. "I thought maybe I could cook, and we could watch a movie or something." He shrugged as if it wasn't a big deal, but in fact it was a very big deal. I'd never been to his place.

"Tonight?" I lifted my eyes to meet his.

"That was the plan, but if tonight doesn't work I could do tomorrow, or the next day." He slowly stood and made his way over to where I was standing. "I want to spend more time with you, and her." His head dipped toward Ava. He lifted his hand and rubbed her soft hair with his palm. "She's getting so big."

"I know. I can't imagine anyone not wanting someone so perfect." I sighed as I watched her close her eyes. She was getting milk drunk, and looked as if she was going to go back to sleep.

"I have to go to work, but I'll come by and pick you up this evening on my way home." He leaned down and pressed a kiss to my forehead. "I'll see you tonight."

"Ok. See ya." I smiled, first at Ava, then at Blake.

oooooooo

Blake called when he was leaving the hospital to let me know he was on his way. When he pulled up to the house, Amy was watching out the window. "He's here." She clapped like a fifteen-year-old.

"Relax. It's just dinner." I shook my head at her. The truth was, I was so nervous I wasn't sure I'd be able to eat dinner. All I kept thinking about was that we were going to be alone in his apartment. I had no idea what to expect. I wasn't even sure how to dress for this. Ava was sound asleep in her carrier. I'd bundled her up, and covered the carrier with a blanket.

"He's getting out." Amy's forehead wrinkled.

"Amy!" I scowled as I lifted the carrier into my arms. I'd already put my coat on. I just had to slip on my boots.

"Hey." She giggled as she opened the door right as Blake was getting ready to knock. His hand was in midair, and the look on his face was priceless.

"How do you do that?" He stared at Amy.

"Super powers." She laughed.

"You ready? I left my car running so it would stay warm." He motioned to the curb.

"Yep. Just need these." I pointed to my boots.

"Let me grab her for you." Blake reached for the carrier and took it from my hands.

"Thanks." I slipped my boots on, and then followed him out onto the porch. "You could have waited in the car. I would have come out," I mumbled as we walked down the steps.

"That is not acceptable. A gentleman never picks up his lady from the car. He always walks her to and from the door." He scowled at me as he secured Ava's carrier in the backseat.

I thought about it for a few minutes. Warren never walked me to and from the car. If he was picking me up after work, he would just honk and expect me to come out. "I'll remember that. Thanks." I gave him a quick peck on the cheek as he opened my door for me.

After slipping in the front seat, I secured my belt and then relaxed back against the warm leather. Soft jazz was playing on the radio, and the only light was that of the street lights outside. Memories flooded me of the nights Warren took me out. Blake had never asked, and I wondered why. Without thinking, the words came flying out. "How come we never go out places for dinner?" My face turned red almost immediately.

Blake glanced at me and then back at the road. "Is that something you want to do?"

"I don't know. Forget I said anything," I muttered as I turned to stare out at the city as we made the short drive. Blake only lived a few blocks away. If it wasn't freezing out, we could have walked.

"No." His voice was firm. "Don't do that."

"Do what?" My head whipped around in his direction. I could see frown lines, and his grip had tightened on the wheel. He was angry, and I wasn't sure what I'd done to cause it.

"Pretend like you don't matter. I want to know how you feel about things. I want to know your desires, your wishes. I wanna know if I do something that you don't like. I want you to talk to me. What you think and feel matters, and you need to tell me even if you think it's something I don't want to hear." He turned quickly and parked in a space. "Do you understand what I'm saying?" He put the car in park, and cut the engine. "There are gonna be times when I get mad, but I'm never going to hurt you. I'm not him, but I am human." He was still holding the wheel and his breathing was ragged. "I'm not him."

"I know." It came out whispered, and I placed my hand on his forearm. "I know."

oooooooo

Blake

I was falling in love with her, plain and simple. I knew when I started this that it would be a challenge. I knew he'd always be in the background, but I guess I didn't realize how hard it was going to be. She's so afraid that she'll upset me, that she won't be herself. "Let's go upstairs?" I opened my door, and then came around to help her out, and grab Ava's carrier. She was awake now, and babbling under the covering Brooke had put on her. "I think she's up." I laughed lightly.

"I fed her before I left, so she should be ok for a little while." She stared up at the building in front of us. "Which one is yours?"

"I'm on the top." I smiled. "Penthouse apartment. I wanted the tall ceilings."

We stepped inside and rode the elevator up. Normally I take the stairs, but Ava's carrier is heavy, and I wasn't sure Brooke would be up for six flights. When we reached the top, I unlocked my door, and stepped back.

"This is really nice." Brooke's voice was shaky.

"Thanks. I need to check the roast, so make yourself at home. Explore all you want." I motioned with my arm as I set the carrier down and closed the door behind us. I went toward the kitchen as Brooke began unbuckling Ava.

"Just toss your coat on the chair over there." I rounded the corner, and left her there. Normally, I'd give a tour, but I wanted to give Brooke time to herself. I could hear her feet padding on the floor as I moved about the kitchen grabbing wine glasses, and putting the finishing touches on dinner.

ooooooooo

Brooke

Blake's apartment was beautiful. His living room had a wall of floor to ceiling windows that overlooked the city. There was a giant brown leather couch that sat to one side, and a large TV on the other. Soft lighting was throughout. A hallway was off to the side, and even though he said to explore, I felt odd meandering through his space. He'd gone to the left when we came in, and I assumed the kitchen was that way. Behind the living space was a large glass table with chrome chairs surrounding it. The walls were white, and everything minus the couch seemed modern. It was as if it was picked out by someone else.

"Hungry?" Blake came around the corner wearing an apron.

"A little," I mused. "You have a great view." I motioned to the window. The snow was still falling softly, and everything outside was lit up with Christmas lights.

"I know." He stared right at me as if the city wasn't even there. "Come on over to the table. I'll get the food. Do you drink wine?" he called out as he was walking away.

"Sure. Anything white is fine." I carried Ava over and nestled her in the carrier, setting it by my feet. If she got fussy, I could rock it with my toes.

It seemed like the evening was going to be perfect, but perfect has never been in the cards for me. Blake rounded the corner carrying a huge platter. Sitting on top of it was a pot roast. There were vegetables piled around. He set it in the middle of the table, and then rushed away before seeing my face fall. When he came back, he was holding two glasses of wine. We sat down, and everything faded away. I was back at the brownstone serving Warren. He was screaming at me that I was lazy and stupid as he used his arm to knock the roasting pan and everything else to the floor. I was crouched on my knees trying to clean up the mess as he berated me and told me I was worthless.

"What's wrong?" I hadn't even noticed Blake move. He was bent over by my chair with one hand on the back and the other on my knee.

"Pot roast was his favorite. I messed it up all the time. I was never right." My voice was monotone as I stared at nothing in particular.

"Fuck!" he hissed. "I should have asked. I'm sorry." He stood, grabbed the roast from the table and rushed back into the kitchen. I heard some banging around, and then he was back with the phone pressed to his ear. "Yep. A large, and put a rush on it." He hung up, and then reached for my hand. "Pizza will be here in twenty minutes. I'm sorry." He pulled me into his chest and wrapped his arms around me. "I'm not him. I promise." He rocked me from side to side, and I think this was the first time that his words really sunk in. He wasn't Warren. He'd cooked a meal for me, and now we were eating pizza because he didn't want me to go to war with my memories. Blake Douglas was slowly winning my heart, I just hoped I was winning his too.

Chapter 23

Blake

The pizza had arrived in record time, and I tipped the delivery boy accordingly. Brooke had been quiet, lost in her head since we'd moved from the kitchen table to the couch. The TV was on, but we weren't really watching it. I was holding Ava and Brooke was just staring off into space. "I'm sorry I ruined tonight," she mumbled without looking at me.

I was shocked to hear the words. She'd been silent for the last hour. "You didn't." I turned slightly, cuddling Ava to my chest in the process. She was sleeping on me, and I didn't want to wake her.

"Yes, I did." She blinked a few times before looking my way. "You cooked a nice dinner, and we ate pizza." She wrapped her arms around her middle, her bottom lip trembling in the process.

"Food is food." I smiled. "Tonight wasn't about what we ate, it was about who I ate it with. I wanted to have dinner with you. I would have eaten chips and an energy drink if that's what you wanted." She started to smile. "You have demons. I know this. I know that I'm always gonna to be fighting them. I know that being in your life means he's in it too; even if he's not there. I get it." I smiled back at her. I get you." I leaned closer and offered a soft kiss.

"Are you real?" She started to cry. "I mean… I just… I've never…" She swallowed before looking away. "You make me want things that I never thought I'd have."

"Like what?" I glanced down to see Ava sucking her thumb. She was drooling in her sleep and leaving a wet spot on my shirt.

"A future." She said the words so quietly, I almost didn't hear them. "I…" It was in that moment that my phone started to ring.

"Sorry." I grimaced. "I have to get it. It might be the hospital." I cradled Ava close as I stood and headed to the kitchen where my phone was charging. When I glanced at the caller ID, it was my brother. I rolled my eyes as I picked up. "Yeah?" Cal never called me at night. He knew when I was off, I was usually asleep.

"I really shouldn't be telling you this, but I feel like you can help me." Cal's voice was hushed and it sounded as if he was cupping the receiver with his hand.

"Ok." I was skeptical. How could I help with anything?

"Is she with you?" He was so cryptic.

"Yes. What is going on?" I was getting annoyed.

"Her ex is out on bail. I don't know how he did it, but he did. The arrest stuck, and he was in county lock up, but his lawyer got him out on bail. I think she should stay with you for a bit. He might come to the house looking for her." There was a door closing in the background. "Fuck, it's cold out!" he hissed.

"Are you off now?" I moved farther into the kitchen. I didn't want Brooke to overhear me. I wanted to tell her all of this in person.

"I'm heading home. I'm going to do a drive by just to make sure he isn't near the house now. He's not supposed to be, but that fucker doesn't care. He thinks he owns her. You should have heard the bullshit he was spouting off in the back of the cruiser when we arrested him."

"I thought you couldn't talk to me about this stuff," I warned. I'd asked Cal about all of this, and he was tight lipped.

"I shouldn't be, but I don't trust him to not try to hurt her." Cal sighed. "I'm exhausted. Been dealing with all kinds of crazy today. What is it with winter and the crazies coming out?"

"I don't know. I see it too at the hospital. I'll talk to Brooke. She's safe for tonight. Tomorrow we'll figure out a plan." I hung up the phone, and carried Ava back to the couch where Brooke was waiting.

oooooooooo

Brooke

"What is it?" I could see the change in his expression almost immediately. Blake never seemed to worry, but right now he was.

"That was my brother." He swallowed as he sat back down beside me. "He was calling about your ex-husband."

"Ok." My heart started to pound. Blood rushed in my ears, making it hard to hear.

"It's gonna be ok." Blake's voice broke through. "You're safe here." He placed Ava back in her carrier on her floor, and wrapped his arms around me. I was shaking, and didn't even know it. "I'm not going to let him hurt you anymore." His voice was hard, like nothing I'd heard from him ever.

161

"Why won't he just leave us alone?" I cried. I was so tired of this. I'd done everything right. I'd left. I divorced him. I didn't ask for anything. I only took clothes with me. I was living without his help. He wasn't even helping with Ava.

"Men like him have a need to control. He doesn't like the fact that he can't control you anymore." Blake began rocking us. "We're going to figure this out. Promise."

oooooooooo

That night, I slept in Blake's bed. He made up the couch in his home office, and he slept in there. I knew it couldn't have been comfortable, but he insisted. Ava slept on a small pallet made up of blankets on the floor beside me. It was one of the few nights that I didn't dream of Warren.

Blake's bed smelled just like him: soap and a woodsy cologne. I snuggled under the down comforter, and stared out the window at the falling snow. I don't know when I fell asleep, but the next thing I remembered was waking up on my own.

I scrambled to look over the edge of the bed since I hadn't heard Ava cry, but she wasn't there. Fear took over and common sense flew out the window. I flung the covers back, and rushed out of the room.

When I reached the end of the hallway, I skidded to a stop, my socks sliding on the wooden floor. Soft music was playing, and Blake was swaying around the room with Ava tucked against his chest. Tears sprung to my eyes. This was something I'd pictured years ago when I'd first thought about having a baby. I wanted to wake up to my husband bonding with our child. I knew that would never happen with Warren, but I'd hoped I could change his mind. Now, it was happening, in the strangest of ways. Here was a man who wasn't my child's father, but he seemed to want to be. He was a natural in every way with her, and my heart opened a little more to him each time he did something like this.

"I didn't want to wake you." He smiled as he spun around, yawning in the process.

"I can take her." I stepped closer and held out my arms.

"It's fine." He brushed me off. "I changed her, and gave her a bottle. We're good." He smiled. "There's some breakfast in the kitchen. Help yourself." He tipped his head to the right.

"Thanks." I shuffled around the corner and immediately smelled coffee. Blake had left a plate of fruit out with some bagels and cream cheese. There was a mug sitting on the counter with a sugar bowl nearby.

"I hope milk is ok. I don't keep cream in the house," he called.

I pressed my lips together to keep from crying. He was going to make me lose it. "Milk is fine," I choked out. I made a cup of coffee for myself, and grabbed a piece of melon. This man was too perfect. Here I was wearing an oversized pair of his scrubs, eating breakfast that he'd prepared, while he took care of my daughter. I almost pinched myself to make sure it was all real.

"Once you're finished, we're going to go back to the house to discuss a plan with Donna. I think Cal wants to make sure that you feel safe there." Blake was now leaning against the counter, watching me.

Ok." I nodded. "It won't take me long to get ready." I finished the melon, and carried my coffee back to Blake's room. My clothes from the night before were draped over a chair in the corner. It didn't take me but a few minutes to dress, and then I was back in the living room.

"Ready." I forced a smile. I wasn't sure how I was supposed to feel about all of this. Scared? Angry? I'd been feeling those emotions for so long that I was tired of them. I wanted to feel happiness. I'd seen it in glimpses, but I wanted more. I wanted a lifetime of it, and the more time I spent with Blake, the more I wanted it with him.

Chapter 24

Brooke

It's been two weeks since Warren got out on bail. It's been rather quiet around here, and dare I say normal. Cal was coming by pretty often, but when Warren didn't make an appearance, he cut back. Blake's been over many times, but he's working a double today. Donna has been even more vigilant, and I rarely leave the house. Roni called just a few days ago, and let me know that the OP had been extended, and to call 911 if Warren showed up. It's made me a little on edge to tell you the truth. As much as I want to make sure I'm safe, I feel like I'm the one who's done something wrong. I'm living as if I'm the one in trouble.

Christmas is in just a few days and Blake has invited me to spend some time with him. I told him I wanted to have Ava's first Christmas morning be here at the house, but I was open to spending time afterwards. He said he understood, but I could see disappointment on his face. It's not that I don't want to spend time at his place, it's just that I feel like the house is my place. I want Ava to feel like she has a home. Donna and I have been discussing what I need to do to get my own apartment. I feel like I need to live on my own for a while before I live with another person. I need to be me, that's something I learned in therapy. I need to build a life that I want, and then if Blake or someone else fits in, great, but I need to be me first.

oooooooooo

"I've got to run out to the store, Amy's here if you need help with anything." Donna was leaning in my doorway. I'd been sitting on my bed with Ava. Donna rarely left me alone lately with the threat of Warren showing up.

"Ok. Don't worry. We'll be fine, won't we, pretty girl?" I cooed as I tickled Ava's feet.

"See you in a bit." Donna smiled back at me before leaving.

We'd made plans for what to do if anyone showed up. We all knew the rules. Part of living in the house is learning how to watch out for one another. We all have our enemies, and we all needed to know who those were. There were steps to follow, and weapons for protection. Donna kept a handgun hidden in the hall closet. We knew where it was, and how to use it. None of us wanted to use it, but it was there just in case. After Donna had lost Emily, she swore she'd never lose another woman and she'd do whatever necessary to make sure that truth held.

I honestly don't remember much about this day. It comes to me in pieces. I'd like to believe it's my brain's way of protecting me. Blake says that sometimes we can't remember things because our mind just shuts it out.

It was around lunch time when Ava went down for her afternoon nap. Amy was in the living room, and I was straightening up the kitchen. We'd done some holiday baking that morning, and left a bit of a mess. I heard the doorbell ring, and Amy call that she had it. I didn't think anything about it. Amy was always answering the door. It was her thing, so to speak. She was like a kid in a lot of ways. She was the youngest of all of us, and seemed to enjoy seeing who was visiting.

This time was different. The usual laugh or teasing response she gave to visitors never came. "Brooke?" Her voice trembled, and I knew right away that something was off.

"Just a minute," I called back. I was drying my hands.

"No, now!" His voice was clipped and a chill ran down my spine.

I dropped the dish towel as a chill ran through my body. He was here. He was going to kill me, and maybe Amy too. I closed my eyes and swallowed as I attempted to control the fear.

Our kitchen had two doors, one that led to the dining room and one that led to the hallway. I slowly moved toward the hallway, sliding my feet along so the floor wouldn't squeak. I knew Warren's routine. I knew that I couldn't give in. I knew that if I did what he asked, he'd assume complete control.

"Brooke!" His voice boomed and got louder. He was inside now, and coming after me. My feet moved faster down the hallway. My hand gripped the closet door just as he reached me. "Where the fuck do you think you're going?" He leaned in next to my ear. His breath reeked of bourbon and he looked as if he hadn't showered in a few days.

"Nowhere," I whispered. I refused to let go of the door, and I prayed that Amy was calling 911. She knew the process. She knew he was here to either take me with him or kill me.

"You're coming with me, you little slut! I've been watching you with that doctor. You spread your legs for him yet?" His grip on my shoulder tightened, digging in. I'd have a bruise for sure.

"Warren," I begged. "You're hurting me," I whimpered.

"Did you think I was here to play nice?" he scoffed. "You've had your fun. Now it's time to go." He started to pull me away, but I fought back.

I was not going to go down without a fight. I spun, and shoved against his chest. He stumbled back, and I used those few precious seconds to stuff my hand between the pillows on the top shelf. My fingers wrapped around the wooden grip, and I spun to face him. "No!" I shouted as I pointed the pistol at him. "Never again!"

"Are you serious right now?" He laughed. He laughed so hard he almost lost his balance.

"Leave!" I demanded.

"I'm not going anywhere without you." His head tipped to the side as a smirk spread across it. "I'm never going to stop coming for you, you know that, right? I'm always going to be there. You're never going to have a normal life, and that doctor isn't going to want you when he finds out how pathetic you are. You're used goods, Brooke. I took what little you had to offer." He sneered.

It happened in a blur. Warren charged, there was a bang and then I saw him slump to the ground. I was still standing there, in the hallway when Cal arrived.

"Brooke? It's over." I looked up to see Cal's face pleading with me. His hand was covering mine and the gun. He was trying to pry it from my grip. "I have to take this." He slowly removed it from my hand. "You're safe. It's over." He said the words again, but they barely registered.

"You should take her and get her checked out." I glanced up to see Blake nodding.

"I got you." His arms wrapped around me, and he started walking me out of the house.

We were halfway down the hall when I turned. "Wait." It was the first word I'd uttered since it all happened. I took a few steps toward his body. Warren was on his back against the hallway wall. His head was slumped to the side. Blood was pooled under him, his eyes were clouded over, but still held malice. How could a human be so evil? What could have happened to him that made him this way?

"I hate him." They were quiet at first, but then the anger came. Donna always said that one day I would find my voice. She didn't know when, but she said it was in there. "I hate you!" I screamed. The tears poured from my eyes. "Why did you hate me? What did I ever do to deserve your wrath? What?" My breathing became labored as I let the anger pour out. "I won. You hear me? I won, not you!" I turned to Blake. "I won." I buried my face in his chest and cried. I'd won. I escaped. I was going to be happy. I survived. I was a survivor, and now my daughter would be too.

Epilogue

1 Year Later…

Blake

Work has been exhausting the last few nights. I've been on the night shift, and Brooke has been working days. We rarely see much of each other even though she moved in with me. We greet each other with a passing hug or kiss as we leave my apartment for our respective jobs, and occasionally she'll meet me during my break for a coffee. I'm counting the days, two more to be exact, before I'm back on days.

It's Christmas Eve, and I managed to work a double so when I go home tonight, I have tomorrow off. That is the one thing that's hard about working in the hospital— you don't get holidays off. We trade off each year so the same doctors don't work the same holidays, unless they want to, and this year I was able to get Christmas off.

"Night, Donna." I waved as I tossed my lab coat and stethoscope into my locker.

"Tell Brooke we said Merry Christmas." She smiled as if she knew my secret.

"Will do." I yawned. I was exhausted, and with the present I had planned, I knew I wouldn't be going to bed anytime soon.

I bundled up, and made my way out to my car. After brushing the snow off, I hopped in and made the drive home. The sun was just beginning to peek over the horizon, and cast a pink and orange glow over the city. The snow glistened and quiet houses would soon be filled with the squeals of laughter as children realized Santa had come.

I pulled into my spot in the garage, and jogged up the steps to the penthouse. All was quiet as I tiptoed inside. I tossed my coat on the chair, made my way into the kitchen, and began brewing a pot of coffee. If she stayed on her usual schedule, Ava would be waking up in the next half hour.

As the smell of coffee filled the air, I shuffled down the hallway. I glanced into my room to see Brooke snuggled beneath the covers. The down comforter was pulled all the way up to her chin, and her brown hair was fanned out over the pillow. It still took my breath away every time I saw her.

I carefully pulled the door to a crack as to not wake her as I turned to head toward my office, now nursery for Ava. When I pushed the door open, Ava scrambled to stand. Her chubby arms reached for the sky as her mouth spread into a giant grin. "Dada!" she cooed as she clapped her hands at me.

"Hey, pretty girl." I moved over to her crib and lifted her out. She was almost fifteen-months-old now and had started walking right around Thanksgiving. "Were you being good and letting Mommy sleep?" I carried her over to the changing table and changed her diaper. I never saw myself as a dad, but ever since I met these two, I've felt like I was meant to be here. This little girl has changed so much for me.

Ava kicked her feet as I worked to get a clean diaper on her. "Dada dada dada." She grinned as her arms flailed around. Every time I hear it, it nearly brings me to my knees. At first I felt guilty. She isn't my daughter by blood. I would never want to take a man's place no matter how awful he is. I was discussing this at work one day, and Donna overheard me. She said that I was chosen to be Ava's dad and I needed to stop feeling guilty, and embrace it. It was my purpose. Donna always knows the right thing to say. She's like a mom to everyone despite the fact that we're almost the same age.

"Let's go out into the living room until Mommy wakes up." I carry Ava down the hall and sit her on the carpet by the couch. After securing a baby gate at the entrance to the hallway, I make my way back into the kitchen to grab a mug of coffee. I can hear Ava babbling in the living room, and the sounds of a few of her toys as she plays quietly. Ava's always been a good baby. Since she was born, she has never really cried and entertains herself really well.

I sat down with my coffee and attempted to read the morning paper. An hour passed and Brooke still wasn't up. "I think we might need to wake Mommy so we can give her our present." I smiled at Ava as my heart thundered in my chest. I'd been putting this off for the last two weeks as I made sure everything was perfect. I plugged in the lights on the tree, turned on some soft Christmas music, and then went to the secret spot I'd picked out in the coat closet. I'd been insisting that I hang up our coats for the last two weeks, and Brooke actually let me. It wasn't until yesterday that she attempted to do it. I panicked and she almost had a meltdown. I wasn't mad, just worried she'd ruin the surprise. She thought I was going to hurt her. It took me an hour to get her to calm down. I felt terrible, but after today it will all be worth it.

I took the baby gate down, and called Ava over. She toddled down the hallway, laughing as if we were playing a game. "Mommy!" I called softly. "Time to wake up." I stopped in the doorway as Ava made her way over to the bed. She wasn't tall enough to climb up on it, so she tugged at the covers.

"Mamama!" Ava squealed, and Brooke's eyes fluttered open. God, she was beautiful.

"Hey, pretty girl." She yawned as she lifted Ava into the bed.

"Hey to you too." I smiled from my spot in the doorway. "Thought you were going to sleep the day away."

"What time is it? Wait! How are you home? Are you on break?" She rubbed her eyes as she sat up, and Ava clapped and bounced from her spot.

"Merry Christmas." I grinned. "Come to the living room. Let's see what Santa brought." I turned and left her there wondering. She knew what Ava had gotten, and the perplexed look on her face was priceless.

It took a few minutes, but soon Brooke appeared with Ava walking just in front of her. "I had her wait to open anything. I wanted you to see it." Last Christmas, Ava was so young that she really didn't understand presents. Now, after her birthday, she knew exactly what presents were for. I'm afraid she enjoys the boxes more than what's in them though.

"Sit." I pointed to the couch, and lifted a large box.

"Is this what's been in the closet?" She smiled as she yawned again. She's been really tired the last few days, but Donna hasn't said anything. Brooke still works at the house.

"Maybe." I chuckled. "Open it."

I could tell by the way she went to lift it that she thought it was heavy, but it wasn't. What was inside was actually really small. She tore into the paper with confusion written all over her face. She rooted around the tissue inside, even more confused. "I don't think there's anything in here." Her forehead crinkled.

"Keep looking," I encouraged. I could tell when she found it. Her entire face and demeanor changed.

"Blake?" Tears welled as she mashed her quivering lips together. Slowly, she lifted the small box as the larger one toppled to the floor.

"Brooke, I've known you were the one since I first laid eyes on you. You weren't mine to have then, but I knew we were meant to be. The first time we kissed sealed the deal, and I've been patiently waiting for your heart to be ready. I love you, and I love your daughter as if she was mine. Spend the rest of your life with me. Be my wife. Will you marry me?" My hand shook harder than ever before as I sat there on the floor in front of her.

"Yes." She sobbed. "Yes." I slipped the ring on her finger, and pulled her into my lap, sealing our promise with a kiss. Ava squealed and clapped in the background as if she knew what was going on. "I have a present for you too." She wiped the tears from her eyes. "Here." She handed me a small box from under the tree.

"You didn't have to get me anything." I took it from her.

"Just open it." She nibbled her bottom lip.

I carefully pulled the ribbon from the box, and lifted the lid. "Does this mean what I think it means?" I held the pregnancy test in my hand. "Are you pregnant?"

She slowly nodded. "Are you ok with that?"

"I'm better than ok with that. We're gonna have a baby." I grinned like a school boy. "My baby's in there." I pointed to her stomach. Brooke's eyes lit up with happiness. "That's why you've been so tired. Donna knew about this." I furrowed my brow.

"I made her promise not to tell." Brooke gave me a guilty face.

"I'll forgive her." I reached over to where Ava was playing. "Come here, pretty girl. Mommy's gonna have a baby." I settled Ava in my lap. "You've got a sister or brother in there." I pointed to Brooke's flat stomach. Ava looked at both of us skeptically, and then without prompting she leaned forward and kissed Brooke's belly.

"I've been dreaming of this for years." Brooke cried. "I've wanted all of this. I love you so much." Her eyes moved between the two of us. She glanced down at her ring sparkling in the light of the Christmas tree before wrapping Ava and me in a hug. "It was worth it. Enduring all the pain. It was worth it for this."

The End

H. D'Agostino

Enduring Act Playlist

You Say- Lauren Daigle
Got it in You- BANNERS
We Are Warriors- Avril Lavigne
Heart Attack- Demi Lovato
Waiting for Superman- Daughtry
Human- Christina Perri
Rise- Katy Perry
Don't Give Up On Me- Andy Grammer
Control- Zoe Wees
Never Be Like You- Flume
Burial- Seinabo Sey

Other Works by H. D'Agostino

The Broken Series
Irreparably Broken
Saving Us
My Broken Angel
Broken Pieces

The Shattered Series
Destined
Shattered
Restored
Renewed
Fated

The Witness Series
Being Nobody
Becoming Somebody
Promise Me Tomorrow
Say You Remember
Below the Surface
Crash and Burn
On Broken Wings

The Second Chances Series
Unbreak Me
The Boy Next Door
The One That Got Away
Inside Out
Fallen from Grace

H. D'Agostino
The Family Next Door

The Cook Brothers Series
Walking Among the Cherry Trees
Beyond the Cherry Trees
Before the Cherry Trees

The Sutter Family Series
Catching Raindrops
Trusting You
Finding the Green Room
Teaching Cayden

Standalones
Privileged
Beautiful Goodbye
Pieces of Forever
Sands of Time
Just One More
One Last Time

The Survivors Duet
Vanishing Act

Acknowledgements

The Survivor's duet has been one of those stories that has been growing in my head for months. I had the idea of some major event pushing someone so far that they'd abandon their life and start new. I wasn't sure what it was that would cause this, but I knew it had to be a big deal. When Brooke began talking to me, I knew I had to tell her story. I wasn't sure where it was going to go, but I knew it was important. I knew that Donna and Blake would play a major role too.

Thank you to my awesome team. I don't know where I'd be without you.

To my alpha, Angie… thank you for not throat punching me over this book. You know I love those mic drop moments, and hearing your reactions show me I got it right. Blake and Brooke needed to have their HEA, and I knew it took a while to happen, but it did.

To my beta, Melinda… see above. LOL You were the reinforcement that I got it right.

To Kellie, my editor… as always, you are top notch. Thank you so much for getting this back to me so fast. From your quick turnaround to your attention to detail, I know that I can always count on a quality product.

To Jimmy and Anna, my patient kids… thank you for all your help on doggie duty. Unfortunately, Luna doesn't understand that Mom is busy. Thank you for all your help taking care of her so I could write.

H. D'Agostino

Last but not least… thank you readers. I couldn't do this
without you. I hope Brooke's story touched you in some way.
Thank you for all you do to spread the word about my books.

About the Author

Heather D'Agostino is an avid reader turned Bestselling Author of the Contemporary Romance Series The Broken Series, The Shattered Series, The Second Chances Series, The Cook Brothers Series, and Romantic Suspense series The Witness Series.

She attended the University of North Carolina at Charlotte where she received a Bachelor's of Arts in Elementary Education with a minor in Mathematics.

She currently lives in Central New York with her husband, two children, dog, and two cats. When she's not writing she can usually be found at the dance studio, soccer field, or one of the many other places that she plays 'Supermom'.

You can follow her here:
Facebook: www.facebook.com/H.DAgostino.Author
Twitter: @hdagostino001

Instagram: @hdagostino001

Website: http://hdagostinobooks.weebly.com

Reader Group/ Street Team on Facebook:

Heather's Hotties:

https://www.facebook.com/groups/877863252256341/

Goodreads:

https://www.goodreads.com/author/show/7034328.Heather_D_Agostino

I love hearing from my readers, so please feel free to reach out.